How Deep Is Your Love

2

Jade Royal

D1446006

© **2018**
Published by *Miss Candice Presents*

JADE ROYAL

Other Works by Jade Royal

- Love is Worth the Sacrifice (Completed Series)
- Two Halves of a Broken Heart
- How Deep is Your Love?

Chapter One

The tears that clouded Charm's eyes began to burn her vision. As they fell all she could do was wipe them away but the tracks of the tears were stained permanently on her face. She sat there stoically trying to figure out what the hell was going on. The doctors and nurses all walked by her at quickened paces not even paying attention to her. The hustle and bustle of the hospital was part of their daily routines. Another crying woman in their midst didn't do much to distract them. It was real hard to believe that someone would have actually shot Terrell out of nowhere.

Charm looked down at her bloody hands and sighed. She tried to scrape the caked blood from her nails but it wasn't going to be completely clean unless she washed them, but at the moment she couldn't even move. The ride to the hospital was chaotic and so fast Charm didn't even register Terrell's injuries. So she had no idea how bad he was and what was wrong with him. And though he was a cheat here she was, crying that he was hurt and now in surgery. Charm's attention shifted when she smelled Denzel's old spice through the thick smell of hospital disinfectant. Unlike her, he was restless. He couldn't just sit there and wait for someone to come out to talk to them. So he'd been walking up and down the hospital halls just to give himself something to do.

Denzel stood across from where Charm sat and looked at her. Her eyes were still glazed over telling him that in her head she was miles away. Her eyes were red and her face was streaked with tears. Denzel didn't quite know what to do. Here he was with the woman who he'd been spending an amazing time with, in the hospital wondering if her ex was going to pull through. Denzel hated seeing her cry, but then again it was tears for the man he didn't want her to be with. But that was selfish of him to tell her not to feel anything for the man she was married to. It just scared him because you just don't stop caring about someone you've been with for that long. He knew it well because while he was angry with Gabrielle he knew that if something like this ever happened to her then he would be just as worried as Charm was over Terrell. He didn't want to just ignore her though because Terrell was involved. Charm didn't deserve that kind of treatment. Exhaling, Denzel leaned off the wall and went back to sit next to her. She jumped out of her daydream, startled.

"It's just me," Denzel said softly. She smiled weakly at him.

"I know," She said lowly. "I smelled your old spice," She added. He sat back comfortably and like it was natural, she scooted next to him and he put his arm around her. She rested her head against his shoulder.

"This is crazy," She said. "I've never been around shooting or guns or anything like that. And this isn't like the gun range."

"I haven't either," He responded. "Has he pissed anyone off lately?"

"Besides me?" Charm scoffed. "I don't know." She shook her head and rested back against Denzel's chest.

"I just want this to be done with and that doctor doesn't come out telling me he's dead or something. He's a cheat but death he doesn't deserve," Charm said after a moment.

"Of course not," Denzel replied. Charm lift her head and turned to look at him.

"Look, about what he was saying about me and him getting back together it's not-" Charm was cut off by her cell phone ringing. She huffed in anger and look at it. She rolled her eyes seeing who was calling.

"Not going to answer it?" Denzel asked her.

"It's Destiny," Charm said. "What the hell she got to call me for? It's clear she got what she wanted out of me."

"I know how you may feel Charm but if she's carrying Terrell's baby then she has a right to know what happened earlier." Charm moved away from Denzel and crossed her arms. She felt like crying all over again just thinking about catching her husband fucking their surrogate. Being with Denzel kept her from sinking into that abyss again but it still affected her when she thought about it.

"She probably didn't even know Terrell was coming to see me to try and get me to come home," Charm scoffed. "So I don't know what kind of relationship she thinks they have." Denzel moved away from her. This was where he was unsure if Charm was seriously ready to move away from Terrell. Not that he was asking her to do it right now, but like he said before it just scared him that he didn't fit into the equation when it came to being with Charm.

"Charm," Denzel said. "Don't be vindictive. She needs to know." She didn't like that he was right but she knew she had to do the right thing. Her phone had stopped ringing so she just called Destiny back.

"You got some nerve ignoring me," Destiny snapped into the phone.

"Whatever Destiny. What are you calling me for?"

"I haven't been able to get in touch with Terrell. He isn't answering my calls and he left bed this morning and didn't say where he was going." Charm shook her head knowing that Destiny was adding that bit of information because she wanted to make Charm jealous.

"Yeah well something happened. And Terrell, he's in the hospital. I'm here with him right now."

"What?!" Destiny screamed. "Which hospital!"

"St. Albans." Before Charm could even finish the sentence Destiny had hung up on her. She sighed and put her phone away. She knew Destiny was going to come up in here chaotically trying to find out what happened. Charm stood and she began pacing this time while Denzel continued to sit. He crossed his arms and just watched her.

"What you thinking about?" Denzel asked her, trying to keep her from going into a tailspin of emotions again.

"Just, I don't want to deal with the drama that she's bringing you know? I'm just here because we were there when it happened. Who knows why that person was shooting in the first place? And now I know she's going to be in here causing a scene and doing a whole bunch of obnoxious shit because of the simple fact that she was able to have his baby and I wasn't." Denzel shook his head.

"You're stronger than that Charm. To let her get to your head."

"It just hurts you know. How can I not be? I can see the cheating, but having her pregnant? It rips me apart."

"Whether she's pregnant or not you can't be okay with him cheating."

"I'm not okay with it!" She snapped getting angry. She paused to take a breath. "I didn't mean to snap at you," She said after she calmed down. Denzel just sat back.

"You're fine," He responded. "Come sit down," He ordered.

"I don't feel like it," She breathed looking away from him. "I'm tired of sitting now."

"Baby girl," He called. She looked at him. He raised one of his brows. "Come sit down." Trapped by his chocolate gaze like a fly to a light, she went directly to him and sat down next to him.

"It's okay to be hurt still you know," Denzel told her. "Like I said to you, no one is asking you to be alright this minute. But just because you're upset doesn't mean that you're weak. So by no means let another woman make you feel deficient in any way." He tugged at her hair to make her look at him.

"I'm talking to you baby girl," She huffed and looked at him. "You hear what I'm saying to you?"

"But Denzel, how long must they have been going behind my back for her to end up pregnant? She only just moved in with us! And if it's so easy for her how come it was never easy for me? I mean I'm the one that wants to be a mother too you know."

"I know that Charm but what can you do huh? Each woman in different. Just because you miscarried doesn't mean you can't get pregnant again. Don't let that woman get to you. And I promise you she's going to try to get under your skin. It's up to you to decide if you want to let that consume you." He ran his hand down her back caressing her slowly.

"This must be so weird for you," Charm said. "To be here with me because of Terrell." Denzel shrugged.

"It is what it is Charm," He said.

"Oh Denzel don't do that," She begged.

"I mean I did catch you kissing him after you fucked my brains out. But that's life," He shrugged. Charm leaned back and gave him the side eye.

"Excuse me?" She asked.

"You heard me," He said looking back at her.

"But I didn't kiss him. He kissed me. Because he thinks that if he kissed me it would have somehow gotten me to remember that we're supposed to be together or whatever he thought that kiss would do." Charm moved Denzel's locks from his face.

"But you said I fucked your brains out," She whispered.

"Is that not what you did?" He asked her softly.

"It was more like the other way around," She admitted. Her

eyes inadvertently looked down into his lap. Denzel shook his head.

"Don't you dare do that," Denzel ordered her. With her just looking at him he knew he was going to get aroused and he couldn't handle that in a setting like this. Especially if they were there waiting to hear what the hell was going with her husband. She shook her head and rubbed her eyes.

"Sorry, I didn't mean to. I couldn't help it." When she bit her bottom lip, Denzel couldn't help but lean into her and place a small kiss on her plump lips. He was ready to pull back just so he didn't go overboard but Charm wasn't having it. She pulled him back and kissed him deeply. Whether she was here or not, the truth was that Denzel still did something to her that she couldn't explain. The taste of his lips seemed to calm her racing heart and allow her to forget anything else that was happening around them. It all evaporated and she just felt like she was alone connecting with the man she found solace in.

"Look at this shit!" Destiny snapped. Charm quickly pulled away from Denzel. Denzel stood immediately just in case he had to keep the two women separated.

"What?" Charm asked standing too.

"Terrell is laid up in the hospital and you out here sucking on another man's face? Are you serious?"

"I know you ain't talking," Charm scoffed. "You must be out of your damn mind." Destiny got up in Charm's face.

"Where's Terrell," She gritted.

"Surgery," Charm answered. "He got shot when he came to see me at work." Destiny gasped.

"So what? Did you plan this because of me and him? Is that what you did?"

"What?! No!"

"Yes you did!" Destiny shoved her finger in Charm's face. Denzel immediately pulled Charm away.

"Look, you're free to say whatever you feel lady, but you gonna keep your hands out of her face," Denzel said stepping into Charm's place. Destiny looked him up and down.

"You're a looker aren't you?" She asked looking him up and down. Denzel shook his head and backed up.

"Ignore her Charm," Denzel warned, seeing Charm fuming behind him. Her cute face was pulled into a deep frown. He rubbed her arms to calm her down.

"Mrs. Robinson?" The three of them looked towards the doctor who was walking towards them. Destiny pushed her way past Denzel and stood in front of the doctor.

"Is Terrell okay?" She asked.

"He's very lucky," The doctor responded. "But the journey is nowhere near done. His internal bleeding has been managed but there are other things as well."

"Can I see him?" Destiny asked.

"Yes, you all can come see him." The doctor turned to lead them to Terrell. Destiny made sure to walk ahead of them like she was running the show or something. Charm just stayed next to Denzel where she felt comfortable.

Inside the hospital room, Charm couldn't help but gasp when she looked at Terrell laying there seemingly lifeless. The ventilator was next to him pumping oxygen into his body. Tears stung her eyes again. Call her soft, but she couldn't see anyone like this and not feel any remorse. He was plugged up to machines, and even though he was unconscious his face was still pulled into a frown. Charm covered her mouth and felt herself moving towards his bed. Next to him she touched his arm. She couldn't believe someone would actually have done this to him.

"Back up," Destiny snapped at her. "You're the reason this happened to him," She hissed. Charm rolled her eyes and moved away. The doctor stood on the other side of his bed.

"The bullet pierced through one of his ribs and glanced off his lungs. Unfortunately he did suffer atelectasis."

"What does that mean?!" Destiny shrieked. Charm was equally worried but she didn't cause a scene.

"It means his lungs collapsed," Charm told her. The doctor looked at her, surprised she knew the term.

"My father was a surgeon before he retired," Charm informed him. He nodded. "But now what? His lung collapsing is near fatal."

"That's true. But fortunately we were able to get him on a ventilator to keep him breathing. The main problem is taking in oxygen. However his ribs did break so they need ample time to heal. We've went in and put a stent in his broken rib so that it sets properly and heals. But some of the main concerns are his breathing. If he's able to get off the ventilator his breathing will still be labored because of the healing rib. He will need to do some therapy to get back to his normal self." Charm rubbed her eyes. At least he was coming out of this alive but she knew Terrell and she knew he was going to hate being seemingly trapped in his own body by not being able to do what he used to do before.

"So what does this all mean? Is he going to be fully recovered?" Destiny asked.

"Yes he will be in time. But for now he just needs support and a lot of it. After he comes off his ventilator he'll need support for daily living activities. And someone to help take care of his wounds." This time is was Destiny shaking her head.

"Well for how long? Because I can't be taking care of no grown man for too long." Charm couldn't even believe what she was saying.

"Um-" The doctor didn't even know what to say to her. He cleared his throat. "We're keeping him until we're confident he can be okay without us. Like I said he's going to need to learn the proper methods to breathing with his broken rib. If not he has a chance of getting pneumonia. That plus we want to watch out for blood clots and on the other spectrum him bleeding out. So we're prescribing him antibiotics, and pain meds." He reached into the folder at the foot of the bed and pulled out papers.

"I also need a signature from his next of kin that will allow us to continue to care for him and do whatever is needed should anything happen during his stay here."

"I'll take that," Destiny reached for the papers but the doctor didn't hand it over to her.

"Um, who are you to him?" He asked.

"I'm his girlfriend. We're having a baby together," She added. Charm scoffed. She doubted Terrell was even going to claim her as his girlfriend but whatever. She couldn't even care in the first place.

"No offence Miss, but-" the doctor looked at Charm. "When you came in with him earlier you said you were his wife."

"I am," Charm said reluctantly.

"So you're his next of kin," The doctor said.

"No, she's not," Destiny snapped. "They're separated. He left her for me so…" The doctor looked between both women.

"Have you filed for divorce?" He asked.

"No I haven't. We're just separated."

"Right. And even if you don't want to Mrs. Robinson legally

you're still his wife so that gives you medical control over what we can and cannot do with him. So that decision rests in your hands."

"Are you kidding me?" Destiny gasped. Charm didn't want to be part of this but she knew that if she just left him she would ultimately start feeling remorseful.

"Okay I'll sign," She said. She took the papers and signed off on everything while Destiny stared daggers at her.

"I don't understand how this is even possible," Destiny finally spoke up. "She may be his wife but she's the reason he got shot in the first place! You can't give her control over his medical needs!"

"You don't even want to take care of him," Charm said rolling her eyes. "How much longer is he going to be out for?" Charm asked the doctor.

"For about another half hour. And when he wakes he's going to be in a lot of pain but now that we have your permission we can administer pain meds immediately." Even though Charm wanted to be there for Terrell, she just couldn't physically be there. At least now she knew he would pull through so she was content with leaving him. Especially since Destiny was going to be there.

"Good. Perhaps maybe I'll come back tomorrow," Charm said. "Or whatever. With his new girlfriend here I don't think he really needs me."

"At least you know your place," Destiny muttered. Charm saw when the doctor shook his head at Destiny, but then he looked at Charm and gave her a curt nod.

"Before you leave let's put your number on file so in case something happens we can give you a call immediately." Charm nodded and followed the doctor out. Destiny watched as they left, giving Denzel a lingering look. Charm sure knew how to choose them. Terrell was handsome that was for sure, but Denzel was another side of chocolate that Destiny would love to devour. But aside from that Destiny hated that Charm was still seemingly in control. Destiny already had Terrell's baby in her stomach. She was always claiming Terrell whether Charm liked it or not and Destiny was determined to get rid of that woman for good.

"I'm sorry for your situation," The doctor commented after Charm gave her phone number.

"Don't be sorry for me. Be sorry for Terrell. He's the one

that has to fight to stay alive right now."

"That is true." The doctor smiled. "I'm going to make sure he stays on the blood thinners so his chances of clotting decreases then he'd be able to go home sooner."

"Thanks Doc. See you again." Charm smiled and waved at him before taking Denzel's hand and walking out.

"You alright?" Denzel asked her as they left.

"Yup. I just need a hot shower and a canvas to calm myself down." Denzel wrapped his arm around her shoulder.

"I got you baby girl." She smiled feeling incredibly comforted.

Chapter Two

"Oh my god! Finally!" Brianna exclaimed when Charm and Denzel emerged through his front door. She was pacing his living room. Ever since she received his text telling her to stay home because there was a shooting she was shitting bricks. Instead of staying home she used her spare key to his place and let herself in to wait for him. He told her he wasn't hurt but she wasn't going to be content until she saw him for herself. So when he came through the door she brushed by Charm and hugged Denzel deeply. She was still a little wary with Charm because of catching her and Denzel in bed so it was a little awkward. Charm cleared her throat and backed away.

"Brie, I told you I'm alright," Denzel said.

"Well I just needed to see for myself. That bullet could have hit you still."

"I'm good trust me," Denzel assured her. Brianna looked over at Charm who was hugging herself.

"Are you alright?" she asked Charm.

"Um yeah. Terrell is gonna make it so at least I don't have to deal with a death right now."

"True." It got eerily silent between the three of them until Denzel spoke.

"You wanna go shower?" He asked Charm.

"Yeah-yeah I do."

"Why shower here? And not at Jason's place or your place?" Brianna spoke up.

"Okay fine. I'll just go. Bye Denzel," Charm said. She just left the drama of Destiny she didn't want to deal with drama with Brianna. She was over the whole drama shit right now.

"Wait," Denzel said. He gave Brianna a look. "I want you here Charm. You know that."

"The last thing I need right now is drama," Charm said. "And Brianna has been by your side for years. I only just showed up. So I'll just do what's right and go." Denzel glared at Brianna. He didn't stop glaring at her.

"Fine!" She snapped finally. "You can stop looking at me like that."

"So stop acting like that," Denzel warned.

"You can stay Charm," Brianna said. "I'm just being bitchy. But you're right there needs to be no drama."

"Denzel can you give us a moment?" Charm asked. He looked between the both of them.

"No. because I don't want you two fighting."

"Come on D. We're not gonna fight. Are you kidding me? We're grown, mature ass women. Get outta here," Brianna said. Denzel gave them one more look before he finally left the women alone. Charm waited until Denzel was out of earshot before she began talking.

"I think I owe you an apology," she said to Brianna. "Maybe I should have told you how I was feeling for Denzel. And then to have you catch us having sex like you did, I know that must not have been fun for you."

"You don't have to apologize to me Charm. You know me and you we're cool. Hell I consider you a good friend. After the way we bonded and how you gave me a job opportunity you know I have nothing against you. But when it comes to Denzel-"

"I know what you mean," Charm cut her off. "I don't know what's happening with me and Terrell. I just know that Denzel makes me feel a way that my husband never has. And then when he cheated I just-the only person I could seek comfort from was Denzel. And after what Gabrielle did to him, we just kind of erupted in all this passion and we couldn't stop ourselves and the sex just happened. And well, I enjoyed it. I don't take him for granted I promise you that."

"Wait, what did gabby do to him?" Brianna asked. Charm pursed her lips.

"He should be the one to tell you," She finally spoke. Brianna nodded.

"The only reason I may have been upset with you Charm is because I know how Denzel really feels about you. And I'd be damned if you play with his feelings by fucking him today and going back to your husband tomorrow. And I know you may feel as if you're never going to take Terrell back but I know marriage ain't easy. And who knows, you could end up wanting to just forgive him and take him back. Denzel doesn't deserve that." Charm felt like a horrible person. At that moment she knew she didn't want to take Terrell back. But what if shit changed? What if she just forgave him down the line and decided not to go through with a divorce? So in a sense, Brianna was right to be upset with her.

"I don't know what I want Brianna. But I know that Denzel makes me feel like the queen my husband is supposed to make me feel like. And I'm just going by what I feel right now. Nothing more, nothing less."

"Listen, I'll let you two do what y'all feel like doing. Who am I to get in between that? But I will tell you Charm even if you're my home girl now, Denzel comes before anything else. So if you do something to hurt that man I just might have to lower myself to an immature female just to fuck your ass up." Charm crossed her arms.

"Or you can try," Charm countered. Brianna smiled at her.

"Glad we got that sorted out," Brianna said. "Denz! You can come back here now." A few minutes passed before Denzel came back to the living room shirtless. Charm was suckered in again, unable to focus for a moment.

"Charm said that Gabrielle had done something to you. What is she talking about?" Brianna asked.

"I actually don't want to talk about it," Denzel said. "I don't want to get myself riled up again. I never want to have that type of anger around either of you." Brianna knew it had to be serious because Denzel knew how to control his anger now. So if something really got him riled up then that something must have been a big deal. And he was right, she didn't want to see him that angry. It frightened her.

"She did slap me though, so if you see her and want to return the favor for me. Be my guest," He added.

"I told her about putting her hands on you," Brianna said shaking her head. "Watch when I see her."

Charm looked at Denzel and smiled weakly. Even though she wanted to get some painting done, she was beginning to feel her fatigue. After the shooting, they had spent literally all morning and some of the afternoon in the hospital. Even though it was only a little after 5, Charm felt incredibly exhausted. But with Brianna there she realized she hadn't even texted Jason to let him know she was alright.

"I forgot to text Jase," Charm sighed.

"Don't worry about it. You look beat plus you did say you were going to take a shower," Brianna said. "I'll tell Jase everything is good."

"Thanks," Charm smiled.

"Come on," Denzel said jerking his head in her direction. She followed him after a moment. He was leading her towards the bathroom.

"Remember I'm here!" Brianna called after them. "If you have to fuck make it a silent one!" Both Denzel and Charm chuckled as they locked themselves in the bathroom.

"I was not thinking about getting a fuck," He reassured her. "Arms up." She lifted her arms in the air so he could take her shirt off.

"Oh sure," She giggled. Denzel unsnapped her pants and pushed them down her legs. She braced herself on his shoulders and stepped out of them.

"You were the one giving me bedroom eyes in the damn hospital remember that," He said.

"Only because you made me," She replied. Denzel gave her a look as he slid by her and went to turn on the shower.

"How in the hell did I do that?" He asked. Charm shrugged.

"You reminded me about what you did to my body and well, I couldn't help it." Denzel tested the water, and seeing that it was warm, he opened the glass door all the way. But before he allowed her to step into the standing shower he reached behind her and unclipped her bra then let it fall between them. Her chest was rising and falling deeply as she gazed up at him. He didn't dare break eye contact with her as he hooked his thumbs into her underwear and slid them down.

There she stood completely naked in front of him and Denzel felt like it was the first time he was seeing her naked body in the first place. He ran a fingertip up her stomach and in between her breasts. Her body involuntarily shuddered at the feeling as her head fell back and a raspy moan left her throat.

"What I did to your body?" He asked her leaning forward and running his tongue along her exposed neck. Her knees trembled so she grabbed hold of his shoulders so she didn't fall over. He nipped at her neck before kissing her chin. He pulled her head down and pecked her lips.

"You know well you did as much to me." He drew her bottom lip into his mouth and pressed down with his teeth. He caressed her supple buttocks in his palms and then squeezed. He moved towards the front as if he was going to dip his finger into her heating walls, but then he moved away abruptly.

"Don't let all the hot water run out," He said nodding over to the shower. Charm stood there, breathing hard feeling like a release was just at the edge of her body. She gave him a piercing stare before stumbling towards the shower.

"Stay with me," She called out as she closed herself in the stall.

"I'm here baby girl." Denzel just leaned against the wall and watched through the frosted glass as Charm showered. He was captivated by her hair, her lips, her lines, everything about her. And to think he'd already had her under his body writhing and moaning in passion as they orgasmed together.

Charm could feel the heat of Denzel's stare through the high temperature of the water beating down on her skin. Somewhere deep inside she felt guilty for knowing Terrell was in the hospital but she was at another man's home bathing in his shower and wanting nothing more than to feel his touch. But on the other hand it was more present in her not to feel anything towards Terrell. She was upset, and she cried, and she prayed that he didn't die but just because she did those things meant that she wanted Denzel any less. Her marriage with Terrell was completely crumpled and she couldn't face being with him again for the hurt that he caused her. So right now, she wasn't his wife no matter what legal papers said.

"Denzel," She said softly.

"Yes baby girl?" She opened the shower door and motioned for him to come inside with her. He was already shirtless from before so all he had to do was take his pants off and come in the shower with her.

"I don't know," He said hesitant. He knew she probably wanted the comfort but Denzel knew if he got into that shower with her and touched her naked body his control would snap. He was already teetering on the edge as it was.

"Don't make me beg," She said.

"I don't think you understand what will happen if I come in there with you. And I don't wanna make you feel like-" Charm waved him off and stepped out of the shower dripping wet. She sauntered over to him and even in her shortness she wasn't afraid to stand toe to toe with him. She didn't break eye contact as she unbuttoned his pants and pushed them off his lean hips roughly.

Denzel just stood there amused that she took control of the situation. He stepped out of his pants, and did the same when she pulled at his underwear. The only time she broke eye contact was when she looked down at his growing arousal. She wrapped her hand around the base and held onto it for a moment. She swore she could feel his heart pulsing through the veins spread out on his thickness. Tugging on his arousal lightly she coaxed him to following her back to the shower. He followed with no hesitation since he didn't want her to yank at his dick any harder. Once inside the shower she shut the door and looked at him while still caressing his wood.

"I don't really like when you tell me no," She pouted.

"I was just trying to warn you Charm." She splashed water all over him, getting him wet. She ran her hands all over his body ensuring that not an inch of him was dry. Once she did that, she wrapped her arms around his neck. And seemingly as if they were one mind, as she wrapped her arms around his neck, he reached behind her thighs and hoisted her up. Ever so delicately, he lowered her onto his aching shaft. Her muscles trembled as he pushed his way into her deep channel. Seated on his shaft, she threw her head back as she moaned in delight. All Denzel could do was groan. Slowly, he began pumping in and out of her allowing her walls to massage his shaft in a way that no other woman had before. He stood under the spray of water loving the sound of it slapping against their fleshes as he pumped into her. Her rough spot rubbed against his sensitive tip. She dug her nails into his shoulders and brought her head forward to kiss him sloppily. He slapped her ass through the spray of water. That seemed to trigger her orgasm. Her body went shock still as her muscles clenched his shaft. The heat of the water seemed cold compared to her scalding insides. She felt too good but Denzel wasn't getting the leverage he wanted.

He shifted and put her against the wall. He continued thrusting up into her. Snaring one of her breasts in his mouth, he sucked and thrust at the same time. Her moans began to bounce off the bathroom walls. Denzel let out a guttural groan. He let her breast pop out of his mouth. He was about to burst as he felt her muscles tightening again. He grabbed both of her butt cheeks and held it tight as he pumped into her. She screamed out his name as she began to come again. Her toes curled up, and her eyes went to the back of her head. He slapped the wall next to her head and slipped out of her weeping core even though he really didn't want to. His orgasm spilled out of him in spurts sliding down both of their wet bodies. Charm held onto him as her body went limp. She didn't understand how he could make her this weak. And she didn't want to compare him with Terrell, but she couldn't help it. She enjoyed sex with Terrell but this thing with Denzel was on a different level.

Since she was still limp in his arms, Denzel held onto her and brought her under the spray and began washing her body. She reached in between their bodies and massaged his softening shaft. His tip was so sensitive his knees nearly buckled.

"You want us both to fall over?" he chuckled. Charm smiled and kissed him softly. She shimmied down his body and helped him wash up so they could both finally leave the shower.

He wrapped her in a large towel then donned one on his own waist before they both left the bathroom. They could hear Brianna on the phone with Jason so they kept moving towards Denzel's bedroom. She wasn't shy about stripping herself from the towel and walking around him naked. Denzel didn't mind her nudity whatsoever but it was distracting as fuck. And even with Gabrielle, he could practically ignore her when she was naked if he wanted to. But there was no ignoring Charm. And she was by no means a super model or anything, she had curves and her breasts had a little gravity in them because if its supple size but it still captured Denzel's attention. The way her skin glowed just made him forget anything that didn't have to do with her.

"You know, I told you about the way you look at me," Charm said as she moisturized her skin with his lotion. He snapped from his daze and acknowledged she was speaking.

"You might just have to get used to that," He admitted. "There's no way I can look at you without staring." They'd literally just had sex and Charm wanted more all because of the way his eyes grazed over her body. It was true when she said that not even Terrell looked at her the way Denzel did. Not even when they first got together did Terrell show her that much attention. Charm turned away and ignored Denzel's lusty gaze so she could get dressed. If she kept paying attention to him, the both of them weren't going to be able to leave the room for the rest of the night. She went into his underwear drawer and pulled out a pair of boxer briefs and threw it at him.

"Please put that monster away," She said looking over her shoulder and seeing his wood start to slowly rise. He chuckled and winked at her before putting his underwear on. He donned a pair of shorts to go with it but that's all he did. Charm was still naked as she was moisturizing her whole body. She had limited clothing items at his place, but she did have clean underwear. And when she bent over to put her underwear on she felt Denzel's hands rubbing against her ass.

"It's so soft," He said lowly.

"Denzel," Charm groaned. She stood and turned to face him. But he didn't answer her. Instead he lowered himself to the ground in front of her. He pushed her legs open softly and delved his tongue in between her folds. Charm moaned loudly and bent over at the pleasure. She speared her hands through his locks and held on tightly.

"Why do you keep coming back?" She gasped out, tossing her head back as her eyes rolled to the back of her head. She wasn't complaining about his desire but if they didn't get ahold of their hormones they would be having sex all the time.

Denzel growled into her folds sending her further into ecstasy. Even with her standing he didn't let that stop him from delving deep into her folds. His tongue invaded her opening digging deep until she was falling over with pleasure. He held her up and continued sucking the honey from her sweet pussy. Her body shook and convulsed in her orgasm. Denzel wanted to just leave it at that but he just couldn't. He stood and picked her up by the waist and carried her over to the bed. He dumped her towards the edge of the bed and pressed her legs against her chest. In one motion he pulled down the front of his shorts and underwear revealing his raging arousal. Charm's eyes were still closed as she had yet to recover for her orgasm. She was so wet Denzel couldn't pass up the chance to be inside her again. He didn't think he could ever pass up a chance to be inside her.

He ran his tip against her folds to coat himself with her juices before he began sliding into her slowly. Even though he was going slowly he didn't stop until he was embedded deep inside her. She was still tight even from her orgasms but her body didn't resist him. Her eyes remained closed as he filled her up. Denzel loved the look on her face as he began to pump into her again. Her mouth opened slightly and her head tilted back. She began to slap at his chest and he didn't realize why until she let out a long cry. Another orgasm blasted through her. The tsunami that happened within her made

Denzel's back bow. He clenched his teeth and fought through the sudden onslaught of pleasure. His senses were overloaded but there was nothing he could do. She just kept coming and coming and Denzel couldn't even describe how good she felt anymore. And he didn't want to hold back. She squeezed her muscles and that had Denzel erupting. He pulled out quickly emptying himself on her womanly core.

"Shit," Charm groaned as she shuddered. Orgasms like the ones she was having should be against the damn law. Denzel let her legs go and fell back against the nearest wall trying to regain his breath. All Charm could do was lay there in complete bliss.

"I'm all tapped out for the rest of the day so please," Charm spoke. "If we keep going like this you're gonna wear out my damn pussy." Denzel chuckled and stood from the wall. He retrieved the damp towel he had around his waist and cleaned her up. While she was still laying down Denzel retrieved her underwear and put it on for her.

"I can never promise I'm not going to come back for more," He said smiling at her. Charm sat up bringing them inches apart.

"Did Gabrielle keep up with you like this? Because I know I can't! It's actually a little weird because I haven't been with-" Denzel moved away from her and wiped his own shaft before fixing his clothing. Charm realized then that he got uncomfortable with her mentioning of his ex. In hindsight now she felt stupid for bringing it up.

"Sorry," She whispered reaching for her bra so she could finish dressing.

"No need for that," He said.

"I shouldn't be mentioning her to you. Especially after we just had sex. Twice." Truth be told the reason he had a problem even thinking about Gabrielle was because he had to force himself to keep his anger in check. Because when someone mentioned her all he could think about was her saying that she aborted his baby and said nothing to him. Even if their relationship was in the dumps he wasn't going to be no deadbeat. And he damn sure would have enjoyed seeing her grow plump with his kid. But she didn't even give him that damn choice.

"Denzel," Charm called snapping her fingers. He blinked and looked at her realizing he'd zoned out.

"My bad, what?" He grunted.

"Nothing," Charm said giving him a look. She went into his drawers and pulled out a clean t-shirt and then put on one of her leggings. She attempted to walk out of the bedroom but Denzel grabbed her arm to stop her. He pulled her into his body and kissed her deeply before letting her go. Instead of continuing to walk she stood in front of him and ran her finger down his chest.

"It's okay to be upset about it," She said. "Remember what you told me earlier. So if you want to talk about it then talk to me. Don't hold it all in."

"I can't talk about it," He gritted. "Because I'm not just upset Charm."

"Yeah well the first night we made love Denzel you were able to talk about it. You told me that I brought you down from the depths of your anger. So don't be afraid to talk to me. Because I'm not afraid of your anger Denzel." She poked at his chest with her finger before giving him a look then continuing out of the bedroom. Denzel stayed where he was for a moment just thinking. He didn't want to be upset around Charm and he definitely didn't want to talk to her about his ex-girlfriend anymore. He wanted to move on and just let Gabrielle go. Shaking his head he finally left the room after finding a t-shirt and putting it on. When he entered the kitchen Brianna was sharing out some food and scolding Charm.

"When I said no noise I meant no noise!" Brianna said wagging her finger at Charm like she was a child.

"Now how awkward do you think it was for me trying get this food going and hearing moans and 'oh Denzel', 'fuck me, oh my God'," Brianna mocked. Charm nearly fell out of her chair doubled over with laughter.

"That is not how I sound!" Charm cried. "Plus I wasn't saying any of that!" Denzel made his presence known by chuckling.

"Oh and you," Brianna said looking at him. She made her voice deep to mock him. "Damn Charm you feel so god. Fuck uh," Denzel shook his head.

"I was not saying any of that," He grunted. He sat around the table where she placed a plate of food in front of him. As he began eating, Charm reached over and pushed his locks out of his face. He gave her a warm smile after looking into her soft gaze.

"Alright stop that lovey dovey shit in front of me," Brianna said. Denzel kissed the back of Charm's hand.

"Eat baby girl, you need it." Charm nodded and began eating.

When she finally looked at her phone she saw the messages from Jason. She sent him a reassuring text to tell him she was alright and Terrell was fine. He was upset with her because he was out of the loop but he would get over it.

Charm finished up her food and while Denzel and Brianna joked and talked with each other, she retreated to his spacious living room where she got out some paint and a blank canvas just to do some painting. She was in her own zone when Denzel and Brianna joined her. No one needed to speak. The good thing about being all three of them being artists was that they understood how to give each other company without having any words being spoken. It seemed like they spent hours in the room together just painting before Denzel's doorbell rang. All three of them looked at each other.

"Expecting someone?" Brianna asked him.

"No. Did you tell Jason to come over?"

"He's planning this thing for his job so he couldn't when I asked him earlier."

"I swear it better not be Gabrielle," Denzel grunted.

"No, let it be her. So I can slap the taste out of her mouth." Instead of the doorbell this time, there were three booming knocks against the door.

"Denzel Johnson! L.A Police! Open up!" They knocked again. Charm gave Denzel a worried look.

"It's fine," He said standing and walking towards the door. "Stay here," He told both the women. He went to the door and opened it. Two police officers were standing in the doorway.

"Can I help you?" Denzel asked. When Terrell was first taken into the hospital he'd already given the cops his statement and they wanted his address and a number to reach him if anything. But now they were at his doorstep so something must have happened.

"We're looking for a Mrs. Charm Robinson. Is she here?" Charm heard them say her name. She stood to go out to the door but Brianna stopped her.

"No. Stay right here. Let Denzel handle it." Charm swallowed the lump in her throat and nodded. She stayed back and just listened to what they had to say.

"Why are you looking for her?" Denzel asked them.

"We'd just like to talk to her. We went by her home and she's not there, and she's not with one of her known friends either. So we received a tip that she's here."

"A tip from who?" Denzel asked.

"We're not at liberty to say. So we need to speak to Charm right now. It's about her husband." One of them pulled out a warrant and tapped it against Denzel's chest.

"Either she comes out or we come in to get her." Denzel took the warrant and looked at it.

"Are you serious right now?" Denzel asked looking at the search warrant for his home. Even if he lied and said Charm wasn't there, they would trash his whole house and find her.

"Very serious," the cop said. He pushed Denzel out of the way and entered the home.

"Hey! What are the grounds for this warrant anyway?!" Denzel shouted after them. But they didn't answer. They went straight to the living room where Brianna was standing in front of Charm.

"Charm Robinson, come with me," One of the cops said.

"Why?" She asked.

"You're needed for questioning in the attempted murder of your husband. You can come willingly or by force." He pulled out his handcuffs.

"What?" She gasped. "Are you-are you arresting me?"

"Depends on how you'd like to follow us to the station." Charm stood there dazed and confused. And because of her silence the cop stepped forward. He pushed Brianna out of the way and roughly grabbed onto Charm. He turned her around ready to cuff her.

"Wait, whoa!" Denzel shouted. He grabbed Charm away from him. It was clear they had no choice in the matter but Denzel wasn't going to stand by and just let them put handcuffs on her. Especially when she didn't deserve it.

"Just relax!" Denzel snapped at them. "She's going to go willingly. No need for the damn cuffs."

"Good choice," The cop said. He took ahold of Charm's elbow.

"Denzel," Charm gasped. "I-I'm scared. I don't want to go."

"It's going to be alright Charm. I'll be right behind you." He clasped her face in his hands and kissed her lightly. The cop began to lead her away.

"I'm right behind you I promise," Denzel called after her. Charm looked into his determined eyes trying to take something from them to keep her strong as she was led away forcefully by the police.

Chapter Three

Charm sat alone in an interrogation room twiddling her fingers. Actually being held in the back of a police car shook her up, but now being alone in the room waiting for someone to come in to her was even more frightening. She didn't know what was going on, but she knew it couldn't be good. When the door finally opened, Charm sat up quickly. She brushed the sweat from her temples and looked at the burly cop and detective that entered.

"Sorry for the wait Mrs. Robinson. Can I get you anything?" The detective asked. The cop stood off to the side and said nothing. So it looked like it was going to be Charm and the detective speaking.

"First you can call me Charm, or you can call me Ms. Bradley. I'm supposed to be getting a divorce. Me and my husband separated."

"Oh well whatever you like. I'm detective Joe. Would you like some water?" Charm shook her head harshly.

"Can we get to the point here? I was dragged all the way over here now someone needs to tell me why!"

"Let's keep calm," Joe said. He leaned forward and opened up a file. Charm got a peek and saw it was photos of the scene after Terrell was shot.

"So you're getting a divorce huh?" He asked. "Can I ask why?"

"Because he's a cheating bastard." Charm spat. Joe ran his hands through his beard. He was old so Charm already knew he was going to be biased simply because he was raised in a different era. In that time it was always the women's fault. And his next statement proved her right.

"So you weren't also having an affair with a Denzel Johnson?" Charm shook her head.

"Actually I wasn't. And quite frankly who I sleep with is none of your business."

"You're very right about that. But yet still you were aiming to divorce your husband because he was sleeping around. So what? You figured the divorce would be too complicated? Thought maybe killing him would be the best thing?" He asked.

"What are you talking about?! Are you accusing me of trying to kill my husband?! Because if you are you better bring some substantial evidence to support that!" She shouted.

"Evidence huh?" He asked. He flipped through the file some more. "Oh here it is. You've have 4 miscarriages correct?" Charm just stared blankly at him. He just kept talking.

"So you've had four miscarriages. And didn't you and your husband hire a surrogate to help you start a family? Didn't your husband find out about your affair and decided to have his own affair with a woman that was trying to do her part in helping save your marriage? And now isn't that same woman pregnant with the baby you've never been able to give your own husband? So what, now he wants to live a happily ever after with her and his new baby but you can't allow that can you?" Charm felt the sting of the tears. They dripped from her eyes and down her cheeks.

"You've been separated how long? Three weeks or so? There's no evidence of a file for divorce. And isn't your husband a wealthy real estate agent? So you realize if you get a divorce and he brings your scandal to light you will walk away with nothing. So the next best thing. Use a divorce as a cover story and kill him for having his affair." Charm couldn't believe how he was possibly concocting this story.

"With him dead and you still legally his wife, then everything will go to you. And with him gone you'd be able to continue your torrid affair. But my question is, were you ever thinking about getting rid of the woman and her baby too?"

"You're a horrible man," Charm breathed.

"But at least I'm not a murderer."

"I didn't murder anyone!" She snapped. "And case you haven't figured it out I was standing right behind him when he was shot! And if he was shot in the chest how could it have been me that did it?!"

"So then who'd your hire to take him out? Or was it your boy toy that knew someone from around the way to help with the crime?"

"Around the way?" Charm asked. "What do you think he is? Some sort of reformed criminal or something? That he knows all the gangs up and down the streets of L.A?"

"He's got that look don't he? What's it you people call it? Locks?"

"You're a racist son of a bitch," Charm snapped. Joe smiled at her.

"Yeah well that's the way of the world ain't it? All this black on black crime and I've got to be the one here figuring out your sick murder plots. So call me all the names you want, but I will get you for this, and you will be locked away for the rest of your natural born life." Charm just looked at him not sure what to say next.

"The surrogate is ready to testify against you Ms. Bradley. And as we speak the police are searching your home. In a matter of time we'll have your arrest warrant and you're going to get locked up." The door to the interrogation room opened.

"Sir, the second suspect is here. He's in room 1," An officer informed Joe.

"Actually, bring him into this room. I'd love to see them try to lie while sitting next to each other. Certainly none of them have their stories right yet."

"Second suspect?" Charm asked. And before she could ask another question Denzel was being pushed into the room with him.

"Mr. Johnson. Have a seat." But Denzel didn't sit.

"Am I being arrested for something?" He asked.

"Son, if you were being arrested you would have cuffs on you," Joe replied. "It's alright. I know you all aren't that bright."

"Really?" Denzel asked. "Well how about this for being bright," He sneered. "Are you, or are you not arresting me?" Joe didn't answer.

"I came down here to get Charm. So if you're not going to arrest me and I'm not willingly giving you any information so technically you can't keep me here. And if you plan to arrest me Detective then I suggest you get an arrest warrant." Denzel looked at his watch. "And seen as the D.A is probably home by now having dinner with their family you ain't getting no warrants tonight."

"Think you're so smart huh?" Joe asked. "We have ample evidence to arrest her! So if you don't want your little harlot in jail tonight I suggest you back the hell up and calm down."

"Charm let's go," Denzel stated. Charm stood slowly unsure if she was really allowed to leave.

"Did you not just hear me?" Joe asked. "Are you deaf?"

"Arrest her?" Denzel snapped at him. "Go on. I'll wait." No one made a move. Denzel looked at his watch signaling his was waiting.

"Oh wait! That's right," Denzel spoke. "You can't arrest her. Because all the supposed evidence you have is circumstantial. So until you have physical evidence Detective, you can't keep neither of us here. She came down there to answer your questions not be accused of a crime she didn't commit. Since you have nothing to hold us on, then we're leaving. Charm come." Charm moved from the table and went to Denzel immediately. She was in awe of his fierce determination to get her out of this mess. And even if it was the police he wasn't backing down not one bit.

"You come near her again without an arrest warrant I'm going to file a complaint against the department and get a restraining order against you."

"Just who the hell you think you are?!" Joe gritted. Denzel smirked at him.

"I may be black you KKK supremacist, but I know my damn rights. And after my people fought to get it, I damn sure ain't never gonna forget it. So have a good night with your bobo the clown looking ass." Charm gasped and forced herself not to laugh. Denzel grabbed Charm's hand and led her out of the room. They walked in quick strides out of the precinct to where Brianna was already waiting in Denzel's car for them. Charm stopped the momentum in the parking lot.

"Charm we'll talk later we gotta go now."

"But what you just did I-I can't believe it," She gasped.

"Yeah me either and technically he can come out and still arrest my ass without a warrant if he feels like it," Denzel said.

"So how come he didn't arrest either of us just then?"

"Cops won't arrest you once you know your shit Charm. Plus he doesn't have any concrete evidence. If he did he would have arrested you with or without the warrant."

"And you know all this because?"

"Are you kidding me? Do you not know who Detectives Benson and Stabler are? They the ones who taught me about the law. Now come on let's get out of here before Bobo comes out here tryna pick a fight again." Charm laughed and him and followed to the car.

"What happened in there?!" Brianna asked as Denzel peeled out of the parking lot.

"They're trying to pin me with attempting to kill Terrell! He concocting this whole story saying how I hired someone to kill Terrell because Destiny is pregnant and I don't want the divorce because I was going to lose everything and I wouldn't be able to get any of his money. But I swear it's not true! I mean, who could I have possibly gotten to try and kill him? And Denzel they were saying that maybe you knew some thug that would have done it all because we're black! And apparently they're doing this big search at my house! And they said Destiny is willing to testify."

"Of course she is," Brianna shook her head. "So what they got evidence or something?"

"They don't have nothing physical," Denzel said. "But I wouldn't put it past them to turn anything into something it's not just to get you. I don't know what that detective's deal is but he wants us both arrested bad."

"And it's not because he cares about Terrell either," Charm scoffed. "He just wants someone in jail." She crossed her arms and shook her head.

"So what the hell do we do now?" Brianna asked. Charm gasped.

"Wait, I need to go home. He said they had a search warrant for the place. It's probably trashed by now," Charm said.

"Where do you live?" Denzel asked ready to head in that direction. Charm just directed him on where to go instead of giving him the address since she doubted he'd even know where it was.

When they pulled up to Charm's house she saw the evidence that cop cars had been there. The front lawn had tire marks all over it. What was wrong with them? Did they think she was hiding a room full of guns or something? Charm got out of the car and looked at the flowers she'd planted that was trampled now. She shook her head and continued up the driveway to the house.

Denzel followed behind Charm looking at the large house looming ahead of them. He never spoke finances or anything with Charm but apparently Terrell was making good money to have them in a house like that. It almost made Denzel feel like he lacked something because of the little loft he owned. But Charm loved his place and she hadn't turned her nose up at it like Gabrielle had. But still coming from something so large was daunting for Denzel.

They all went into the house and saw the disarray left by the police. It looked like a hurricane ran through the house.

"Shit," Charm said looking around the place. She almost wanted to cover her eyes she couldn't believe it. When they got to the living room Charm looked up when she heard footsteps coming down the stairs.

"What are you doing here?!" Destiny screamed. "If you touch me I'll call the cops! They told me what you did to Terrell!" Charm crossed her arms and stared at her. The woman was a good actress. But Charm wasn't falling for that.

"Drop the act," Charm snapped. "I know it was you that called the cops and told them the bullshit about me being responsible for Terrell getting shot. Now I'm in deep shit with the cops why the fuck would you do that?"

"I just gave them the answers to their questions," Destiny shrugged. "I'm pregnant you're not, and now you're bitter. I get it. So I told them that. Is it not true?"

"I swear something is wrong with you," Charm shook her head.

"Oh you," Destiny said nodding towards Denzel. "What do we call you?" She trotted down the rest of the way and walked by Charm and stood in front of Denzel.

"You were a little mouthy in the hospital but you ain't so bad on the eyes," She bit her lip and looked him up and down. Charm felt a feral heat pour through her. She was ready to snatch the back of Destiny's head when Brianna stepped in front of Denzel and pushed Destiny back.

"It don't go down like that with this one," Brianna said. "Touch him and it's me and you, you psycho." Destiny rolled her eyes and turned back to Charm.

"Well now that you're here you might as well get to cleaning," Destiny told Charm.

"Excuse me?" Charm questioned.

"Start cleaning this shit up. What you expect me to do it or something?" Destiny asked. "I ain't no damn housewife."

"You got some nerve," Charm said. Destiny gave her a look and smiled at her.

"I'm gonna go take a bath in the master bathroom, then I'm gonna visit Terrell. So get to it. We don't want him to come home to a messy place now do we?" Charm raised her hand to smack fire out of her when she felt Denzel's strong hand around her wrist. He jerked Charm back and tucked her against his side.

"Stop," He whispered in her ear. Charm tried to fight to get out of his hold. She was through taking shit from Destiny.

"Let me go," Charm gritted.

"You can't touch her. She's pregnant, remember?" Destiny stepped up in her face.

"Right. I'm pregnant! And you better not forget that. I'm giving your husband something you could never. So you better fucking respect me. Try and touch me again Charm, and I'm getting you arrested for assault. So try me." Charm just looked at her. Destiny laughed in her face then turned on her heels and walked back up the steps. Charm watched her go feeling powerless to even say anything else. She snatched herself from Denzel's hands.

"Let me go," She snapped. "You know I wanted to smack the shit out of her why you gotta block me for?!"

"You heard what she said?" Denzel asked. "First, she's fucking pregnant you can't put your hands on her. And secondly you see how fast she brought up the cops? She can have you arrested in under five minutes and if it gets to that I won't be able to help you like I just did. I told you not to let her get under your skin. Every time you turn around she's gonna be there. And in time she's going to be carrying around a belly. You need to let it go Charm."

"Says the guy that won't even say his ex's name because then he'll get pissed off," Charm said. Denzel gave her a sour look. She realized then she probably shouldn't have said it, but she was blinded by anger for that moment.

"Are you good here?" he asked. "Because I don't have to be here if you don't want me to be."

"No, I want you here," Charm said lowly. "I just, she can't be allowed to talk to me like that!"

"She's immature. Leave her there. Queens don't lower themselves to that kind of shit. I already told you that." Charm crossed her arms and even though he was right Charm didn't want to hear it.

"And I'm supposed to just stay here and clean all this shit up by myself," Charm pouted.

"Don't even trip on that Charm. She's a bitch but I still got your back I'll help you out. After all this is still your home. I can call Jason too I know he'll help," Brianna spoke up. Charm looked and Denzel. She appreciated the help but none of it was going to matter if Denzel wasn't staying too.

"Do you still want to leave?" She asked lowly. He tilted his head and looked at her. When he didn't answer her, she walked towards him then put her arms around his waist and hugged him.

"Don't leave," Charm said rubbing her face in his chest. She looked up at him, giving him the best puppy dog eyes she could muster. He looked down at her his face was stern.

"Those ain't gonna work on me," He said.

"Are you sure?" She asked in a baby voice grinding against him and showing her pearly whites. His façade finally broke and he smirked at her.

"Oh get off me," He smiled. He removed her hands from around his waist. "Let's get started then. Someone call Jason and get his butt over here. It's mad shit to do." Charm went on her tippy toes and kissed Denzel on the cheek.

"Thank you," She smiled. She got ready to clean to huge mess left by the police while she called Jason to come over.

By the time Jason came over everyone was elbow deep in the mess. So far the kitchen was clean and they were working on the living room. Jason dove right into working while Charm and Brianna filled him in on what happened with the police. Denzel stood off to the side picking up the picture frames that were tossed off the mantle. It really didn't make any sense that they trashed the place like this. It was clear they were given a specific order from that damned detective. It frustrated Denzel that this was something added that they had to deal with instead of trying to figure out who fired the shot in the first place. Lost in his thoughts, he bent over and picked up the last photo on the ground. His thoughts derailed when he turned the photo over and saw it was of Charm and her husband together. They were sitting outside and Charm sat in between his legs. He was leaning forward so they were cheek to cheek and the both of them were smiling. Denzel didn't know why he couldn't stop looking at the photo. Jealousy and both fear crept into his body. He was jealous of Terrell for even being married to Charm in the first place, and then he was fearful because Denzel didn't want to lose what he had with Charm because of Terrell. He was so stuck staring at the photo he didn't see when Charm came up next to him, but he felt when she hugged him from behind. She peeked out from behind his back and looked at the picture in his hands.

"I remember that day like it was yesterday," She said softly.

"Looks like you two were real happy," Denzel stated. She scoffed.

"On this particular day we had an argument. I told him I was lonely and that I wanted us to spend some more time together. I packed up a basket so that we could go to the park and enjoy some wine and cheese. And you know what he said?" Charm shook her head and scoffed again.

"He point blank told me no. He said he had clients and didn't have time to play around."

"Wow," Denzel said.

"So I went to the park by myself. Couple hours later he shows up because he's worried about me. Then he sits with me for two seconds and wants us to pose for a picture so I did. And that's that."

"So why do you look so happy if you weren't?" Denzel asked.

"Because he was my husband. And I thought I had to look a certain way. His coworkers thought I was this amazing wife and I wanted to keep that image. I didn't dare want to give people the idea that sometimes I was unhappy so I just faked it." She let her arms drop from around him and took the frame from him. She went into the back and pulled the picture from the frame. Denzel watched as she looked at for a while. He wanted to ask her what she was thinking but before he could she sighed then ripped the photo in half. Denzel gave her a look but she didn't say anything. She tossed it in the trash and walked away. Denzel didn't want to pursue the topic but her ripping that picture apart meant something serious.

Chapter Four

Charm's eyes were heavy as she pieced back her bedroom. She stuffed her shoes into her closet and heaved over. She was beyond exhausted and she had no idea what time it was. Destiny never came back after she left to go to the hospital so Charm was relieved of that. While she was cleaning up the master bedroom she saw the evidence that Destiny had been staying in there. Her panties were thrown about the place and so were her clothes. But on Terrell's side everything was neat and in its place like it always was. Even though he was a man he didn't like mess, and even if things were messy there was a certain organization to it that he understood.

But clearly despite her uncleanliness, Terrell was still shacking up with Destiny. And strangely, Charm didn't care. She was hurt of course to the point where she actually want to put her hands on Destiny. But that was more for the lack of respect Destiny showed her. But knowing she and Terrell were still having sex just solidified the fact that Terrell had made his choice and it wasn't Charm. But then again, Charm had made her own choice too. And it wasn't Terrell. Charm stood slowly and left the bedroom. Down in the living room Brianna and Jason were sleeping on the couch.

"Denny?" Charm called through the house quietly so she didn't wake Brianna or Jason. She didn't hear Denzel answer but she spotted the patio doors slightly open. Figuring he must have went outside, Charm went in that direction. Sure enough, he was standing in the backyard looking out at the sky.

"Denny?" He acknowledged her call this time and turned to look at her.

"That's a new nickname," He smiled at her. Charm walked over to him slowly. She engulfed herself in his warm embrace when she got close to him. He held her in front of him and wrapped his arms around her body.

"You okay?" He asked kissing her cheek.

"Yeah. Just real tired. What time is it?"

"Around 2 am or so."

"Shit," Charm mumbled. Denzel moved his hands to massage her shoulders. Charm's head fell back loving the feel of his hands on her body. That plus she had some serious kinks in her shoulders. But the massage swept her into bliss and before she knew it she was literally asleep on her feet. She started to fall back but Denzel's strong chest kept her protected.

"Baby girl you're beyond tired," He whispered.

"The massage just feels real good," She replied with her eyes closed. Denzel looked over into her beautiful sleeping face. He ran his fingers over her cheeks and then pushed her hair behind her ear. The silkiness glided through his fingers.

"You're so beautiful," He said lowly. He didn't know why he didn't expect her to hear that but the moment he said it, her eyes popped open and she looked right at him.

"There you go staring at me like that," She said. Things like telling her she was beautiful, or just looking at her the way he did always reminded Charm of why Denzel and Terrell were different. Maybe because she actually married Terrell he figured he didn't need to do any of that stuff anymore. And even Charm didn't realize how much she appreciated those sentiments until Denzel began doing it.

Denzel moved swiftly and hoisted Charm in his arms. He carried her back towards the house. She immediately snuggled against his chest on the verge of sleep again.

"You should eat something," He said to her. "We didn't have anything since you were taken in by the cops."

"I'm not hungry," She whispered.

"And I'm not asking you to eat baby girl. I'm telling you that you need to eat. So just stay awake a little bit longer so I can get you some food." Charm groaned. She didn't want to stay awake any longer. She wanted to stay curled up against his chest listening to his heart beat, lulling her to sleep. But Denzel walked straight to the kitchen and plopped her down on one of the stools around the island. He shoved a boatload of mail in her direction.

"Check your mail. You haven't been here since when." He was right. She didn't even think to check it. While she did that, he raided the cabinets and the fridge to see what he would whip up for her. But everything was literally empty. Except for the eggs.

"It is after 2 in the morning. So you won't mind an omelet right?" he asked her.

"Anything you make for me is fine," She smiled at him. He nodded and took out the eggs. He found some green peppers, onions, and cheese. Since none of them had eaten, Denzel made everyone their own omelet. When he was nearly done he didn't hear Charm rifling through the mail anymore. And sure enough when he turned around she was leaning her elbow on the island with her face in her palm fast asleep. He smiled and shook his head.

"Baby girl," He called her. She jumped up and nearly fell off the stool. Denzel dove to catch her. Her chest rose up and down hard as she registered where she was.

"Sorry," He said. He righted her on the stool before picking her up again and carrying her to the living room. He sat her next to Brianna softly. He left her there to return back with the plates.

Charm took the plate from him. She had to admit that it smelled pretty good and she was hungry enough to devour the whole thing. After giving her the food he moved over to Brianna and shook her lightly.

"Brie," He said softly. She slowly blinked open her eyes. "Sorry to wake you but I want you to eat something. Come, sit up." Charm watched the tender exchange between the two best friends and she just had to smile. Whether it was her or Brianna and she imagined with Gabrielle too, Denzel was about the most caring man she'd ever encountered.

"Thanks Denz," She smiled at him. "I was dreaming about food too." Denzel smiled at her and plucked her nose before going back to the kitchen. He emerged with the third plate for Jason. But instead of a tender wake up call, Denzel kicked the bottom of the chair he was sitting on.

"Aye wake up," Denzel said. Jason jumped up and looked around ready to fight whoever had stirred him from his beauty sleep. His eyes went right to Denzel. But Denzel gave him a cheeky smile and held out the plate for him.

"Rise and shine!" Jason sniffed at the omelet and took it without complaint. He didn't hesitate before he started eating it.

"You're lucky I was hungry anyways," He grumbled.

"Yeah, yeah, yeah," Denzel smiled at him. Lastly, Denzel went back to the kitchen for his plate. When he returned, Charm was just looking at her food not eating it.

"What's the matter?" Denzel asked her. But she didn't answer. He leaned over to get a good look at her again. He thought she was just looking down at the food but instead her eyes were closed again and she was sleeping.

"Charm!" Her head snapped up. She rubbed her eyes.

"I'm up, I'm up," She said. But her tone was groggy.

"I said you need to eat. Stay up for a few minutes and just eat the damn thing."

"It's not my fault you know! You gave me like what, fifty thousand orgasms just hours ago. I'm fucking beat." Denzel rolled his eyes and went over to her. He took her plate from her hands then made her stand up. He took her place and sat on the couch then pulled her to sit in his lap. He set his own plate on the coffee table and held her plate in her hand then began slicing up the omelet. Charm watched in awe as he forked some up and aimed the fork at her mouth.

"Open up," He ordered. She opened her mouth and allowed him to feed her. He sat back shifting her comfortably in his lap and fed her slowly. Charm felt like such a baby for him having to feed her like this but the worse part of it was that she loved it. And when the food was done she was leaning back on his chest with a full stomach feeling content. Denzel watched as Charm's eyes closed as she rested back against him. He put her plate down and got his plate so he could eat himself. As long as Charm was taken care of then Denzel was fine.

He ate his food and by the time he was done, Charm was sleeping against his chest again snoring lightly. Neither Jason nor Brianna had fallen back asleep so they were sitting up watching her.

"You need to get some sleep too," Brianna said to him. "You should be just as tired."

"I am," He sighed. Brianna took his empty plate from him, then took it with hers and Jason's and Charm's to the kitchen. With his hands free he was able to stand keeping hold of Charm. He hoisted her up comfortably and started carrying her towards the stairs.

"Um, where are you taking her?" Jason asked.

"To her bedroom," Denzel said.

"I wouldn't suggest that," Jason hinted.

"Because?"

"She hasn't been back here until now since she left. And I doubt she'd want to wake up without you, and in the bed she shared with her cheating husband."

"Yeah but we just spent all these hours cleaning up the damn house. I thought after that she'd want to stay here at least for one night knowing Terrell won't be here."

"She only cleaned up all this stuff because it's still her stuff. Even if she split with Terrell this is a home she took years to build. She wouldn't just leave it. But hey you can leave her here and try your luck in the morning or you could bring her back to your loft and spend the night with her like I know you want to do." Denzel stood there for a moment considering what Jason was saying. Charm was the perfect weight in his arms and Denzel barely felt a strain to hold her for a moment.

"Okay my place it is," He finally decided. He didn't even know why he had to think about it. When he looked down into his arms at Charm's sleeping face, he felt his heart flutter a way that it had never done before. Even if he didn't quite know what was happening with them he just knew it was deep.

Chapter Five

Terrell blinked his eyes open for what seemed like the tenth time. But before each time he opened his eyes, they were drawn close again as if his lids were weighed down by cement. This time however, his eyes remained open. Everything around him was blurry but by smell alone he knew he was in the hospital. Pain was slicing through his ribs and chest. Wait, was he alive? He blinked again and tried to move. He felt his arm moving but almost as if it wasn't even attached to his body. He groaned in pain trying to look around. Through his blurry vision he saw someone sitting next to him. The person stood and hurried out of the room. When they came back, someone else was with them. Terrell could see the white lab coat so he figured it was the doctor.

"Terrell can you hear me?" he asked. Terrell nodded. The doctor checked the machines next to him.

"I'm going to remove him from the ventilator. Let's see if he can breathe on his own." Terrell closed his eyes as the doctor began turning off the machine's next to him. Another nurse came in to help the doctor get the tube out of his throat. He clenched his eyes tight at the pain of the tube being removed.

"Deep breath in Terrell," The doctor ordered. Terrell took as deep a breath in as he could and the doctor pulled the tube from his throat. Terrell immediately went into a fit of coughing when the tube came out, blood and mucous came up his throat. The nurse cleaned him up.

"This is a good sign," The doctor said. "That he can cough and mucous can come out. But he'll be in some pain. But welcome back. You've been out for a week." With the tube out, Terrell just wanted to know if his wife was there.

"Charm?" He croaked out.

"Do I look like Charm?" Destiny snapped at him. He rubbed his eyes and blinked some more.

"Oh." Terrell couldn't hide the disappointment he felt at knowing Charm wasn't the one that was here.

"Don't sound so excited!" Destiny scoffed. "Not like I'm the woman carrying your baby or anything." Terrell groaned when he tried to take a deep breath and all he felt was zinging pain through his ribs.

"Sorry I was just shot," He replied dryly to her. "But how are you?"

"Been sick a few times but that's to be expected." Terrell didn't reply to her. Instead he just turned his head and looked out the window. The sun was just starting to rise behind the horizon but that veil of nighttime wasn't completely gone.

"Did Charm come and see me?" Terrell asked without looking at Destiny.

"Why do you care?" Destiny asked opening up a magazine. "She did leave you and doesn't have intentions of coming back." Even if that's how it seemed, Terrell wasn't going to stop trying to get his wife back.

"Does she at least know I'm still alive?" Terrell asked.

"Yup. Apparently she's your next of kin. You know I find it so unfair that I'm the one with your baby and the one you chose to be with and I can't have a say in how to take care of you." This time Terrell snapped his head in Destiny's direction. The notion caused pain to rip through his body.

"Fuck!" He cursed, closing his eyes and groaning. After composing himself he tried to breathe again and looked at Destiny.

"I never chose to be with you Destiny," He told her firmly. "You know I want my wife."

"Didn't feel like that when you were fucking me against the wall," She commented.

"Just because I wanted to fuck you Destiny, doesn't mean that I want you." Destiny rolled her eyes. She knew he would put up a fight but once Charm was out of the picture Destiny knew he would want her. That plus she was sacrificing her damn body for his bloodline.

"Wow okay, so should I just set up an abortion appointment and fuck off from your life then?" Destiny stood throwing down her magazine.

"No!" Terrell shouted. He was struggling to breathe as his temper began to rise.

"Terrell?" Destiny realized she was putting him into a fit. The doctor had never left so he was there immediately to get the situation under control.

"Calm down," He said smoothly as the nurse got ready to put something in his IV.

"I'm giving you pain medication," she informed him. "It might make you drowsy but that's better that getting you riled up by anything. You really need to take it easy." Terrell felt the drugs immediately.

"I implore you Destiny, that you need to keep him as comfortable as possible. We cannot afford for his lungs to re-collapse." Destiny just sucked her teeth.

"Someone call my wife," He muttered. "Please. I need her here."

"Don't worry I will," The nurse said. Even though he was whispering Destiny heard everything Terrell said. When the nurse and doctor gave him one last check and left the room, Destiny approached his bed. She leaned over and looked at how the medication began to take hold of him.

"You want her here yet she could have been the one to get you shot in the first place," Destiny said. Terrell acknowledged her.

"Impossible. Besides, Charm can't stand to live without me. She may be upset now but she's gonna come back. Because where the fuck else is she gonna go?"

"This poses a dilemma for you Terrell," Destiny said. "Because you want her, and yet I'm the one carrying your first child. You're a high commodity it seems."

"What are you talking about?" Terrell slurred as he began falling asleep.

"It's all in your dilemma. You want Charm. I want you. And someone wants you dead. Too bad that someone might actually be that bitch you call your wife. Because who the hell else would want to kill you more than her for finally being able to have a baby but not with her? Thank about that." The meds began to kick in high gear and Terrell felt himself falling asleep, but not without first questioning for himself who in the heck tried to kill him in the first place.

****

Gabrielle paced her bedroom. It felt like she hadn't left her house for days even if only one had passed since she ran away from the scene of her crime. She slapped her forehead. What was she thinking? Trying to kill someone? Was she crazy? Gabrielle stopped pacing. She turned and looked at the medication bottle on her night table. She charged towards it and just stared at it long and hard as if she was trying to impose her superiority over it. But with what happened just recently she knew she wasn't superior to anything. And if she didn't find a solution and quickly she was going to end up in jail. Mashing her hands together, she dug her nails into her palms as she thought about her only options. Cursing she went to her bed and picked up her cell phone. She looked at Denzel's number for a while. She almost hit send and called him but she changed her mind at the last minute. Denzel would hear from her but she had to get herself together before she did. He would know something was wrong immediately if she wasn't her usual self. So instead she looked up another number and quickly dialed it.

"What?" The harsh answer was nothing Gabrielle wasn't used to.

"I need your help," Gabrielle whispered.

"With?"

"I hurt someone. And if they know it's me I can end up in jail. I-I don't even know if they're dead or not." There was a silence.

"Have you been taken your medication?" Was the next question.

"Um, no. I-I couldn't."

"Then I can't help you Gabby!" She snapped. "I told you to stop calling me every time you get yourself into trouble because you don't want to be on your medication. This whole thing may have worked with our mother Gabrielle but it won't work for me. Especially after what you did the last time I helped you. I have a family now. And I cannot be dragged into these dangerous things that you do. Stay on your medication and you will be fine!"

"You're no help!" Gabrielle shouted. "Just make sure my money is in my account like it's supposed to be!" She hung up the phone quickly. She knew her sister would refuse to help, but Gabrielle had to try. The last time her sister Gemma offered her help to get out of a bad situation Gabrielle had an outburst that constituted in her hurting her own niece. When she was in her right frame of mind, Gabrielle understood why Gemma refused to help her anymore. But that didn't stop Gabrielle from calling her whenever she needed the help. But she hadn't seen her sister in years. They communicated over the phone and through bank transfers. When their mother died, Gemma was left in charge of the money they inherited because she was the so called sane one. And every month Gabrielle received a large sum of money to keep her on her feet. That's what paid for her place, her clothes, jewelry, and all the fancy shit she wanted.

And that's why she got so pissed when she thought about all the shit going wrong for her. She had money, she was gorgeous, and she knew how to fuck; Denzel could attest to that. So she didn't understand why she wasn't getting anything that she wanted, when she wanted it and how she wanted it. There was no one else in her life. No one except Denzel. And then this crafty bitch just shows up and tries to take the only person Gabrielle has left? No, it wasn't going down like that. Gabrielle punched her headboard. The wood splintered her knuckles making her cry out. She shook her hand out and looked at her bleeding knuckles. Her anger turned into shock as she stared at what she did to herself. Huffing she stood from her bed and grabbed her pill bottle. If she was ever going to figure this shit out she needed a clear head. She popped her pill and swallowed it without water. These things worked when it wanted to. And when you were bipolar, sometimes shit never seemed to want to work when you needed it the most.

Gabrielle looked at herself in the mirror. She checked to make sure she had no blemishes on her face, that her hair was perfect, and that she hadn't gained any weight. After checking her figure she looked at her undamaged hand. She was wearing the promise ring Denzel gave her. The night she blew up on him about getting her a newer promise ring instead of an engagement ring was because she thought she'd be okay for the night without taking her medication. In fact, she didn't think she needed it. She'd been doing so well without it. And then boom, Denzel just went and did something so stupid like not proposing to her in the first damn place. She never wanted to exhibit any of her bad behaviors towards Denzel. For ten years she'd been hiding her disorder, and she was going to keep it that way.

Looking at her dresser she spotted the photo of her and Denzel at their senior prom. She went to pick up the photo and looked at it deeply. She remembered the first time they met. She was standing at her locker when someone inadvertently bumped into her. The first thing Gabrielle did was turn around and push the person back. But the person she pushed back barely moved. He looked at her, pushed his short dreads from his face and flashed her his pearly whites.

"Sorry pretty girl," He said winking. He gave her a long look before he eventually walked off. And in just that moment Gabrielle knew she wanted him. And whatever Gabrielle wanted, Gabrielle got. And she didn't stop until she got Denzel. And she didn't see the need to tell him about the medication she took to keep herself in check. He didn't need to know. And once she had her nails embedded deep into him, he was whipped and wasn't going anywhere. But it made it all the worse now that he was refusing to marry her. And despite the pill she just popped her anger started to reheat.

"Ten fucking years and all he wants to do is give me a damn promise ring!" She screamed. "Oh, you're gonna fucking marry me. Watch. I will not lose you Denzel. Not to another woman." Gabrielle rubbed her palm against her head as a headache began to infiltrate. She knew Denzel was going to be hers but if her ass landed in jail then that wouldn't be possible. So besides staying out of jail, the only thing she was worried about was getting Denzel back. And now she was truly regretting aborting his baby. That would probably be her only ticket to get Denzel back easily. But even if it was hard now, she wasn't giving up. What was important was that she had to take her time. If she showed her face to Denzel right now he'd probably knock her head clean off her shoulders. So now she was stuck in between knowing what she needed to do and not knowing how to do it or even where to start. And it was possible she was going to need help. She just didn't know from who.

Chapter Six

Charm didn't have to open her eyes to know that she was next to Denzel. His cologne was still intensely fragrant even if he wasn't wearing a shirt. Taking in a deep breath, she rolled over onto him on his chest. He stirred a little and wrapped his arms around her body. Thankfully he hadn't kicked her out by now since for the whole week she'd been at his place.

"You okay?" He asked her. Charm just nodded against his chest. She couldn't get enough of him to the point where she just shimmied her whole body on top of him. He grunted when her knee hit him in the balls.

"Damnit Charm," He groaned trying to fix her so she wasn't kneeling in his balls anymore.

"Sorry," She whispered. She shimmied down a little so her privates could match up with his privates. When she looked up, Denzel was looking down at her.

"What is it you're hoping to accomplish by doing that?" he asked her. "Because I know this ain't your way of asking for some dick?"

"No!" She stated boldly. It wasn't her intent to want sex but laying on top of him and feeling his arousal begin to thicken her walls began to coat with moisture. She gave him a look but Denzel was matching it with the look on his face. Charm groaned and sat up sitting directly on his groin.

"I promise I wasn't trying to have sex," She said. "And I mean, if I wanted it I would have just went in and taken it. Simple." She shrugged.

"Simple huh?" Denzel asked testing her. He put his hands behind his head and looked down at her. Charm leaned back and raised her brow.

"Challenging me huh?" she questioned. She shimmied down a little so she could pull down the front of his shorts. Charm bit her bottom lip at his mocha coated arousal. She held the base of his shaft and moved up and down slowly caressing him. When he tilted his head back and bit his body lip it was erotic for Charm, raising her own arousal higher.

She wanted to tease him since he was teasing her in the first place. She bent over and drew the flat of her tongue against the back of his thick shaft. His body shivered under her. And though it was meant to be a tease once Charm tasted a small bit of him she just had to have more. She opened her mouth at his tip and slowly took him in. His stomach clenched as she took him as deep as she could go. But she also didn't want to vomit on him tryna be a porn star so she kept it within her limits. His groans let her know that he was at least enjoying what she was doing. Her eyes burned as she took him in and out of her mouth going as far back in her throat as she could take. Saliva leaked out of her mouth and drenched his thickness as she continued to bop her head up and down swirling her tongue all over him. He grunted and thrust his hips forward stroking her mouth.

"Shit," He gasped. He tried to pull himself from her mouth, but she latched on and sucked her cheeks in. Denzel felt his eyes bulge out of his head as his release began spurting out of him. His body bucked as she held on, continuing to suck pulling out every ounce of his release. Denzel had to physically pry her off his dick before she sucked him completely dry. Charm giggled as Denzel tried to get his composure after ripping her away from him. She licked her lips.

"You taste real, real good," She groaned crawling up his body. She began stroking him again in hopes that he'd start to get hard once more so she could feed her dripping walls.

"Take those off," He muttered trying to pull at her panties. She'd slept in his t-shirt and only her underwear. She was knocked out before they even left her home so she figured he was the one who changed her clothes before putting her in his bed.

Excited, Charm quickly shimmied down her panties and threw them over her head. She grabbed at his throbbing shaft again and even while he was hardening in her hand, he began pulling at her arm to pull her up his body.

"What?" Charm asked confused as to what he was doing. All she wanted to do was climb onto his shaft and ride him.

"Just come here," He coaxed continuing to pull her. She continued crawling up his body but soon there was nowhere to go but over his face. Understanding sparked in her brain at what he wanted. He smirked at her and placed his hands on her ass to help lead her on top of his face.

Seeing her luscious pink lips hovering over his face made Denzel's mouth water. He couldn't wait to have her so he forced her down and began lapping up all her juices like a starved animal. Her body jerked on top of him as she seated herself comfortably on his face. Denzel groaned in the back of his throat as he pushed his tongue down her channel. If he could wake up to this every morning he'd be the luckiest muthafucker on the planet. When he suckled at her clit Charm squealed and locked her legs tight against his head. He was so deep in her pussy he could care less if he suffocated or not. She grinded her core against his tongue to further amp up her pleasure.

Charm pressed her face against his large headboard, scratching at it as he continued to suckle and lap at her clit. Out of the corner of her eye she saw her phone lighting up on the night table next to the bed. She turned and looked fully. She didn't recognize the number calling her so she paid it no mind. She moaned out loud as her orgasm began to rear its head. She closed her eyes but not before she saw her phone lighting up again with the same number calling her back. She slapped the headboard, feeling her legs begin to tremble around Denzel's head. She leaned off the headboard and reached for her phone. But Denzel didn't stop munching on her. Even though she had to lean to the side, moving slightly off his mouth, he followed her wherever she went. He wrapped his arms around her legs to keep his mouth attached to her. Charm grabbed up her phone just as her orgasm reached its peak. Her cry of pleasure was hoarse as her body convulsed around Denzel's head. Her clit was so sensitive she couldn't manage his lingering licks so she fell back completely trying to get away from his tantalizing lips. Laying backwards, Charm just stared up at the ceiling feeling like she just got her soul snatched. She felt Denzel teasing her opening with his fingers.

"Ready for your dick now?" He asked her. Charm put a finger in the air.

"I...I need a minute," She breathed. "Please." Denzel chuckled and caressed her stomach. Charm still had her phone in her hand when it began lighting up again. She raised her hand up so she could see who was calling her again. It was the same number. She cleared her throat so she didn't sound like she just rode a man's face into oblivion.

"This is Charm Bradley," She answered as professional as she could.

"Hello, Ms. Bradley, it's Tina from the hospital. I'm Terrell

Robinson's nurse." Charm wasn't surprised to hear from them but it had been a week and he was hopeful that they didn't need to call her. But nope, here they were.

"Oh, hello," Charm responded.

"Terrell has been in and out of sleep because of his pain killers but he keeps requesting that we call his wife. He's awake now and getting a little bit agitated. Plus, Dr. Murphy wants to update you on his condition. Would you be able to come in?" Charm sat up a little and looked at Denzel who was looking right back at her with concern on his face.

"Um, yeah, sure I can come in. It would take me about an hour or so though so it's not right away."

"That will be fine Ms. Bradley. Thank you so much." Tina hung up the phone and ended the call. Charm sucked her teeth and threw herself back down on the bed.

"I can't believe this," She sighed. She turned over before finally getting up. "I have to go in and see Terrell." Denzel was upset that she had to go of course but he wasn't going to throw a tantrum. He rubbed her arms.

"I know you have to take care of business," He said. "I can't fault you for that." Charm pouted. Was she inconsiderate if she was upset that she couldn't ride Denzel's dick because she had to go take care of Terrell? No doubt he only kept asking for her because he still had this crazy assumption that she would take him back. But he had his new woman and a baby on the way. What the hell did he need her for? Charm was crying when he was shot because she wouldn't ever wish death on someone, but not that he would make it she was ready for them to go their separate ways.

"Don't pout," Denzel said. Charm snapped out of her thoughts realizing Denzel was still looking at her.

"Just have my dick ready when I get back," She said. Saying those words out of her mouth made her feel both empowered and gave her a sense of territory when it came to Denzel. He smiled at her and sat up.

"Sometimes I think you're just sticking around me for my dick," He teased.

"No!" She gasped. "I wouldn't be here if you didn't have the tongue action that you do either," She joked. Denzel gasped and reached for her pulling her down on the bed. He hugged her tightly and nipped at her ear.

"Don't play with me," He whispered in her ear. He held her on her side and spooned her. He lifted her top leg in the air and brought his hips forward rubbing his tip along her folds. Naturally, Charm moaned and tried to push her hips back so he could enter her. But of course because he wanted to be a tease, he slipped his tip inside her and pushed in enough for her walls to be stretched at his entry before he pulled out and let her go.

"Let me get you something to eat before you leave," He said kissing her on the cheek. When he hopped out of the bed Charm sat up quickly and shot him a look.

"Are you kidding me?!" She snapped. He shrugged his shoulders and gave her one of his cute little smirks.

"Remember not to play with me," He warned her.

"But-but you started!" Charm threw a pillow at him.

"But you're not supposed to egg it on," He smiled. "Come on, you gotta get ready." Charm shook her fist at him but he only walked out of the bedroom laughing. She huffed but got up eventually and went to take a shower. Once she was clean, she combed out her short hair before putting it in a short ponytail and letting the loose wisps hang loose around her face.

In the kitchen, Denzel was making her another omelet. The one he made for her at her home was good so she didn't mind eating it again. She sat around the table and watched him. For some reason she was just too comfortable in his presence to be without him.

"Are you busy today?" she asked him.

"Not really," He replied. "I'll probably go to the gallery and do some work."

"Come with me to the hospital. I don't want to be there alone." Denzel turned and looked at her. He handed her the plate of food before pouring her some orange juice.

"Is that a good idea?" He asked.

"Who knows," Charm shrugged. "But I-I just want to be with you. And well, who the hell knows if I'm even strong enough to handle Terrell right now." Denzel gave her a comforting smile.

"I'll come with you," He said. He knew it would probably be awkward, but if Charm needed him he was going to be there for her. Even if they were fucking each other's brains out, he did commit to being her friend and that was more important when it came to helping her deal with something.

While she ate her food, Denzel went to take a shower himself before he got dressed in a simple t-shirt, and dark jeans. Back out in the kitchen, Charm had made him his own omelet so he'd have something to eat as well. He could tell she was starting to be consumed by deep thoughts because she became incredibly quiet and her eyes were always zoned out. Denzel didn't want to force her to talk about anything, but he wanted her to know that he was there if she needed to just let everything flow out. He went to stand in front of her and cupped her face in his hands. He saw when her eyes returned back to normal and she blinked at him. He smoothed her eyebrows down and smiled tenderly at her.

"I'm here," He said simply. She smiled at him and nodded in his hands. She gave him a quick peck on the mouth before he let her face go.

Charm could foresee any kind of drama happening by bringing Denzel along, but she just needed him by her side and he was ready to accompany her. It would never be in his intentions to leave her down and out when she needed him. That was a quality that Charm appreciated in him. So together they drove down to the hospital to get an update on Terrell.

Chapter Seven

Terrell was breathing hoarsely through the pain of his ribs. It was a very unpleasant feeling to have something hindering the way you took breath naturally. Terrell found himself beyond frustrated but it was literally nothing that could be fixed anytime soon. He had to just let his body do the healing but he wanted nothing more to get out of this hospital.

"Destiny," He breathed trying to get her attention. She looked up from her magazine.

"What you want?" She asked.

"Ask the nurse if she called Charm yet." Destiny crossed her arms.

"You out ya damn mind," She snapped. "You wasn't calling for Charm when you was in my pussy Terrell. So now you wanna call for her?"

"Stop saying that!" He snapped.

"You know what it's alright. You'll see that all you're gonna have is me. And since I'm the one carrying your seed I'll always be around. Charm won't show you no damn commitment after this. Just watch." Terrell groaned and turned away from her. He was sure everything Destiny was saying was right, but that wasn't going to deter him from being with Charm. Destiny was almost his fall back. It was like he wanted her around for the sake of his baby but if he could have Charm he was going to have her. And if Charm was being too difficult then he had Destiny to fall back on. The two women needed to be around each other and get comfortable because sooner or later they were going to be living in the same house and Terrell needed some sort of cohesion especially when the baby came.

"I'm going back to sleep," Terrell grunted. His eyes were on the verge of closing when he heard a soft laugh in the hall. His eyes flipped open. After being with the woman for so long, Terrell knew the sound of his wife's voice.

"Charm!" He called out hoarsely. Destiny perked up wondering if Charm was really there. And to her displeasure, Charm and the doctor walked into the room. That sexy chocolate man Charm was with before trailed behind them. Destiny eyed him dreamily. Wicked thoughts on if she could take Charm's next man away from her like she did with Terrell invaded her brain. Destiny had to shake her head to stop thinking about another plot when she was still deep in another one. But she had to admit chocolate man looked like he knew what he was doing in bed.

"We didn't mean to wake you Terrell," Dr. Murphy said.

"It's fine. I heard Charm laughing in the hall." Terrell looked at Charm. She had her hair on one of those messy ponytails she did when she was going to paint. But she was wearing jeans and a blouse that fit her just right. There was a glow about her that made Terrell's heart just clench. It was like the first time he ever saw her. They were only teens but Terrell was convinced she was going to be his wife. And now look at them ten years later, and he'd screwed up tremendously.

"Charm," He breathed. "How-how are you?"

"I'm fine Terrell. How do you feel?" She still had that cold edge to her voice so he knew not even being shot would make her go soft on him from what he did to her.

"As long as you're here I'm fine," He spoke up quickly.

"That's why I was laughing in the hall. Dr. Murphy was telling me you wouldn't stop asking them to call me to come here. I just found it hilarious."

"You're my wife. Why wouldn't I want you here?" He asked. Charm shrugged.

"I could think of many reasons."

"Come here," Terrell coaxed her. She was standing all the way across the room and he wanted to feel her touch. She immediately shook her head however and retreated into the comfort of the man Terrell hadn't even noticed was standing there. He remembered then how Charm was quick to explain to him why she wasn't at fault for Terrell kissing her the day he got shot in front of her gallery. So this was him. This was the man fucking his wife.

Terrell tried to sit up slowly. Both Dr. Murphy came over to his bed to help him sit up and raise the bed to keep his back supported. Terrell pointed an accusing finger at Charm.

"You know you're still my wife right? Any way you cut it, your last name is still Robinson. And you dare disrespect me by bringing that man up in here?" Charm gasped at his words.

"Disrespect?" She whispered. "What do you know about respect Terrell? Or did the definition change sometime over the years and I failed to realize? Is fucking the woman who's supposed to be a guest in our own home respect Terrell? Is having her here right now but begging for the nurse to call me in to see you respectful? You don't know nothing about respect and I'll be damned if you lay there scolding me when you've done your fair share of disrespectful shit."

"That wouldn't have had to happen if you would have been able to give me what I wanted in the first place Charm. So think about that shit!" Charm felt her back bump into Denzel. She turned ready to go, unable to face the accusation Terrell was making. She was never ready to face the accusation of her not being able to carry her own baby. But even as she tried to leave Denzel didn't get out of her way. He held her wrist and turned her back around to face Terrell. He leaned over and whispered in her ear.

"If you run every time he says something to hurt you Charm then you'll be giving him the power to say whatever he wants to say to you whenever he wants to say it. Stand up for yourself." Charm inhaled and let Denzel's words flow through her. She exhaled and this fierceness empowered her.

"You better watch your mouth," Charm said to Terrell. "Because as far as I'm concerned you would have gotten your damn baby if you would have just let things happen like how the fuck we planned it. But because you couldn't keep your damn dick in your pants you needed to fuck around with her. But let me tell you something, keep admitting to cheating because the miscarriage was my fault. Go head. The divorce is happening Terrell. So please give me more shit to tell the judge. Because at the rate you're going, you ain't gonna be left with shit." Charm already knew she didn't want any of his money but she knew that would put fear in his heart. And when he crossed his arms and said nothing Charm knew the message had sunk in.

"Atta girl," Denzel whispered to her. Charm smiled. She did feel a sense of strength at being able to stand up for herself. Dr. Murphy cleared his throat. He was clearly uncomfortable, but then he began talking to get the conversation in another direction.

"So, if Terrell keeps progressing well we'll soon be able to release him. The key now is just watch for pneumonia since his lungs was the most affected by the shooting."

"Which by the way I think Charm is the cause of that," Destiny spoke up. Charm sucked her teeth hard.

"Well the cops want to talk to you Terrell, I've been sending them away because you weren't healthy enough. But if you feel well you can talk with them and clear this whole mess up."

"There's nothing to clear up. We all know who did it." Destiny sang.

"Shut the hell up!" Charm snapped at her.

"Or else what?!" Destiny challenged. She stormed over to Charm ready to get in her face. She pointed her finger in Charm's face.

"You ain't gonna do shit are you? Because you know you fucking can't!" Charm just stood there feeling humiliated by this woman. She felt as if she wanted to retreat again but Denzel stood firm behind her. He reached over Charm's head and slapped Destiny's hand from Charm's face. Destiny gasped, taken aback that chocolate man had hit her.

"I told you before to keep your damn hands out of her face. And I'm not playing around with you." Destiny backed up and just looked him up and down. She turned to Terrell.

"He just hit me!" She squealed.

"Doc, I want him out of here! He's putting his hands on fucking women!" Terrell began yelling and that only escalated his breathing which was already short to begin with. He struggled to get his next words out as pain lanced through his ribs.

"Alright everyone calm down," Dr. Murphy said trying to keep the peace so Terrell didn't further injure himself.

"I said I want him out! How dare you touch her? She's fucking pregnant you asshole!" Denzel sucked him teeth.

"I'm out of here," He grunted. Charm was ready to go with him.

"No Charm! You have to stay!" Terrell snapped at her.

"Stay?"

"Fucking him won't change the fact that you're still my wife. And your rightful place is here next to me. I've been shot for fucks sake! You mean to tell me you're so fucking sprung on the next man you won't even take care of the man you made a vow to?!" Charm was stunned. She opened her mouth to speak but nothing came out. What should she even say? Yes he was shot but what, did that mean she was supposed to be waiting hand and foot on him or something? Was she obligated to do that? Suddenly, Charm began to feel terrible as if she was truly just a woman looking to fuck another man instead of caring about someone who she spent most of her adult life with who was almost killed. As she sunk into her thoughts she felt Denzel grab her arm. He pulled her out of the way and stepped in front of her.

"Are you stupid?" Denzel snapped at Terrell. "You keep talking to her on some she's your wife type shit but another woman just hopped in her face and disrespected her and your ass was fucking silent until I smacked her hands from Charm's face. If you cared so much about your damn vows, no woman, no matter who the hell she is to you would be able to treat your wife like that. And to be real playa, if you can fuck whoever you want to, then so the hell can she. But unlike you, I'm not gonna sit back and let the side bitch talk any kind of way to Charm. Just know that her willingness to be here right now caring about your ass is out of the goodness of her heart, not no fucking obligation. So when you catch some fucking sense she'll come back and see your trifling ass if she wants to." Denzel kept hold of Charm's arm and pulled her out of the room with him.

"Charm don't go!" She heard Terrell call out to her. But that only followed by a bout of coughing. One of the nurses rushed into the room to help calm Terrell down. But Denzel didn't stop walking. He strode with long steps that had Charm jogging just to keep up.

"Denzel, wait," She begged trying to get him to stop. She smacked at his wrist. He stopped abruptly and let her go. When he turned around and looked at her, Charm understood why he was acting like that. The anger in his face was unmistaken.

"I swear to god if he wasn't already in the fucking hospital," Denzel snapped. He punched the nearest wall. Charm jumped but tried to hide it from him. He saw her anyway and glared at her.

"You see why I don't like to do shit that would trigger my anger?" He asked. Unable to stay still he began pacing. "I know it was probably gonna be a whole bunch of shit going on if I came here but for him to talk to you like that? And for him to allow another woman to be all up on you waving her hands in your face like she lost her fucking mind? I don't know what kind of man you been married to Charm, but I don't tolerate that kind of shit. Hell you don't even have to be my fucking woman for that kind of shit to piss me off. You think some bimbo could do that in Brianna's face and I don't say shit?"

"Well if she could even get close enough. Brianna would

probably karate chop her in the face before you would even have to open your mouth." Denzel stopped pacing immediately and turned to look at her. And just like that, he felt his anger begin to rise off his body as he chuckled.

"You're so stupid," He said shaking his head. He stood where he was taking deep breaths to continue to calm down. Charm walked over to him and wrapped her arms around his waist and hugged him tightly. She buried her head into his chest. She had no words to explain to him how much it meant to her that he stood up for her like that. She never expected Terrell to defend her honor especially when it came to Destiny. But knowing that Denzel had her back made her feel safe. Sometimes that's all a woman ever wanted out of a man.

"You really called her a stupid bitch," Charm chuckled. She let go of him and held his hand before they continued to walk again.

"And I don't like using that word on females. But shit, she pissed me the hell off. And I don't mean to push this in your face again Charm, but if I was going to cheat on you I wouldn't do it with someone who didn't look as good as you or better than you in the first place." Charm shrugged.

"Maybe she's just better in bed than I am." Denzel scoffed.

"Maybe on another planet," He retorted. Charm smiled at him.

"I don't mean to push this in your face again Denzel, but Gabrielle is real cute. Very ethereal, and graceful. What if now I'm the less attractive side chick while you got your beautiful woman huh?" Denzel rolled his eyes. He stopped walking.

"That's what you really think?" he asked.

"I don't see you denying it," She replied.

"Okay so first thing, you can't be my side chick because me and Gabrielle aren't together. So that right there doesn't make sense."

"But you think she's prettier than me?" Charm asked. Denzel gave her a look.

"What? Are you insecure or something?"

"I'm just saying," She shrugged. "I couldn't help but think about Gabrielle in a moment where I'm thinking about how protective you are and the fact that she had that all to herself."

"Don't think about Gabrielle in that way. Because I'm not comparing the two of you. But just know that if I didn't find you attractive I doubt that I'd let you nearly suffocate me this morning by riding my damn face." Charm rolled her eyes.

"Fine. You win." He winked at her as they continued walking, finally getting out of the hospital.

"But let me ask you one more question," Charm said.

"What?" Denzel groaned already knowing it was going to be that one question he didn't want to answer.

"Who's better in bed?" Charm asked.

"How'd I know you'd ask me that?" He questioned. "I'll tell you, if you tell me if I'm better than that punk in there." Charm rolled her eyes.

"Well the both of you have very two different kind of dicks. His is more slender but long. Yours is thick but long and you have a fatter-"

"Whoa, whoa stop," Denzel said waving his arms. "I didn't ask for the inside edition of another man's dick," He said flatly. Charm put her hands on her hips.

"The both of you pleasured me but in a different way. But I don't know I guess my orgasms are bigger when it comes to your dick. Your turn." Denzel put his hands in his pockets.

"There is no doubt Charm that you feel incredible. If I was to have sex with Gabrielle right now I doubt I would get anything out of it like I get with you. But I still haven't had sex with you in a way that's meaningful enough." Charm was taken aback.

"Excuse me? I don't understand. I'm giving you my body and that's not meaningful enough for you?!"

"I don't mean it like that." Charm crossed her arms. Denzel knew if he didn't explain himself in 2 seconds he was likely to get kicked in the nuts.

"We're just fucking each other Charm. Fucking because we crave each other sexually. Fucking because we share a connection with piece of shit ex's. I'm not saying that everything we do is pointless. Are we having sex because we're going to be together? No. We're having sex because it takes away from the pain of what we've been through. Do I want you? Hell yeah. Do you want me? I would sure hope you do. We are literally friends with benefits Charm. I don't know about you, but for me that's not meaningful enough. Because eventually I'm not gonna wanna be just your friend anymore. Sex between fuck buddies and people who are actually falling in love with each other feels different. Do you feel like you love me? From the amount of times we've had sex?" Charm shook her head slowly.

"So what does having sex with me mean to you Charm?" He questioned.

"What does having sex with me mean to you Denzel?" she countered.

"It means that I get a chance to share my body with a woman that makes my heart fluctuate in rhythm every time I lay my eyes on her."

"Having sex with you Denzel gives me a sense of freedom. I know I can walk away from my cheating husband because I know that I can't just have sex with anyone and it be random. But my body craves you."

"That's what makes our sex so damned good Charm. But is that gonna be enough for the either of us down the line?"

"Why did I have to get on my high horse and ask you that question?" Charm asked herself. She rubbed her eyes and walked by him.

"At least we realize I'm not at fault here," Denzel called out. Charm stopped walking and turned around.

"I still get to ride that stallion later right?" she questioned. Denzel smiled.

"As long as I get to taste that sweet pussy again," He murmured. Charm had to look around them to make sure no one was listening or watching them. She crooked her finger telling him to come to her. And when he did they resumed walking hand and hand without a care in the world.

"I think after this we both need a paint session," Charm said. "Plus we need to create new pieces for more of our paint and sip sessions."

"True. We need to actually start scheduling those. I need money," He said.

"Oh shit have you been struggling? I haven't been on top of the company because of all this shit."

"No, no I'm fine. But we should keep the momentum going with hosting the sessions."

"So let's go straight to the gallery. I'll ride my stallion later tonight." Denzel smiled at her.

"I'm satisfied with that," He said. "Let's go."

Chapter Eight

Gabrielle didn't know what to do with herself as the day went on. After being bored with looking at the inside of her home, she decided she wanted to see Denzel. But she didn't want to confront him. She only wanted to watch him from afar just so she could look at him. Just so she could know what he was doing. It was nerve wrecking because if he ever saw her, Gabrielle knew he would throw a fit. But she just had to see him. It was just entering the afternoon hours when she finally decided to just suck up all her nerves and go to his place. Maybe she could just talk to him for at least five minutes and he wouldn't be tearing her head off.

Just to make sure things went well, she dressed casually in a pair of jeans and a tank top. He hated when she dressed too classy to do something simply like grocery shopping. So she dressed in something he would approve of and that would lessen the blow of her presence. She also wore one of her perfumes that he loved the most. She brushed her hair back out of her face and put it into a low ponytail at the base of her neck. She gave herself one final look and was ready to walk out of the door when she spotted her medication. She looked at it long and hard. Did she need it right now? She felt fine and completely in control. Nothing could go wrong right? Gabrielle shrugged and waved off the pill bottle. She didn't need it. Feeling excited and nervous as the same time, Gabrielle left her home and went to go see her man.

She was running on pure adrenaline as she drove out to Denzel's place. The excitement of actually seeing him was building inside her. She was already thinking of how their conversation would go and how she could lead her way into his bed again. She would probably caress him between his dreads like he loved just to soften him up before going in for the dive. When was the last time she was even made love to? Denzel kept her satisfied at all times. But she was in a drought right now. She felt her foot get heavier on the gas. She didn't care that she was afraid that he would blow up on her. If she couldn't handle just looking at him, then she needed to make a move. Only when she finally pulled up to his place she knew he wasn't home. She looked up and down the street for where he usually parked his vehicle but it wasn't anywhere in sight. But just to make sure he really wasn't home, Gabrielle double parked her own vehicle and hopped out. She still had her key to his place so she rushed towards the building and let herself in then took the elevator up to his loft.

"Denzel?" She called out. There was no answer. Gabrielle walked around his place and she heard and saw nothing. She went into his bedroom and halted. What was that smell? The room was neat like he always kept it but there was a hint of something sweet on top of his signature old spice. Gabrielle looked around the room. Her heart rate increased when she found the culprit. On his small sofa in the corner of the room she spotted a pile of folded clothes. On top of the pile was a pair of underwear and a bra.

"Maybe it's just my stuff I left over here or something," Gabrielle told herself. She walked over to the pile of clothes but she already knew it didn't belong to her. Gabrielle clenched her hands into fists to keep herself from damaging anything in his neat room.

"Deep breaths," She told herself. She began to back out of the room so she didn't amp herself up anymore. He was sleeping around and they had barely broken up yet? She shook her head and walked out of the room completely. In his living room her eye caught all his paintings lined up against the far wall. She snapped her fingers. If he wasn't here then he was at that damn gallery again. With that woman. Gabrielle headed out of his place. She knew exactly where to go to next. And if he wasn't there then she'd park right back at his place and wait for him to show up.

That excitement that was bubbling up within her was slowly turning to anger. Denzel had no right to be sleeping around with another woman. Gabrielle had never given her body to another man. Denzel was her first and he was her only. What right did Denzel have to give what was hers to another woman? And that's the exact reason why Gabrielle wanted to shoot her in the damn face in the first place. Gabrielle let out an aggravated sigh as she motored towards the gallery. Gabrielle felt herself teetering on control but she really needed to pull herself together. She just knew if she saw that woman around her man she was going to lose it, but she had to refrain from doing so.

"That's still your man. No matter what woman he's entertaining. He'll always be yours." Gabrielle repeated that to herself as she continued her journey to the gallery.

This time she felt some sort of victory when she pulled up in front of the gallery and spotted his car parked a couple spaces down. No matter how many models of the same car existed in this world, she knew Denzel's car apart from all of them. And it helped to see the paintbrushes dangling from the rearview mirror. Gabrielle found her own parking. Once she was settled she took a couple deep breaths to calm herself down. This encounter may not be pleasant but she needed to keep her head in the right space. If she did that she would be fine.

The curtains were closed like they always were so Gabrielle couldn't see inside. She cleared her throat, stood straight and knocked on the door.

Both Charm and Denzel looked at each other. Anyone they could be expected would have had a key to come in themselves instead of knocking. They'd arrived at the gallery only 20 minutes ago and hadn't even began painting yet. They were looking through the list of possible events that Jason had compiled for them.

"I wonder who?" Charm asked. Since she was closer to the door she got up to answer it.

"No I'll get it," Denzel popped up. He wasn't quite comfortable with Charm answering the door and none of them knew who was behind it. He stepped in front of her and went ahead to answer the door. Charm followed close behind him and stayed at his back when he opened the door. Denzel had to do a double take. One because he wasn't expecting to see Gabrielle, and two because he didn't recognize her because of how she was dressed. He looked her up and down captivated by the fact that she actually looked…normal.

"What are you doing here?" Denzel asked sternly. Charm felt Denzel tense up. She immediately began to rub his back to try and keep him calm. Gabrielle saw Charm and for a moment all she could do was see red. She couldn't speak, she couldn't even think.

"Gabby," Denzel snapped his fingers in her face.

"Um-" Gabrielle was trying to remain in character and not completely lose it.

"I think something is wrong with her," Charm said. "Let her come in." Despite what Denzel felt, he moved to the side as Charm took Gabrielle's hand and pulled her inside. Denzel closed and locked the door once she was inside. Gabrielle snatched her hand from Charm's hold. She blinked her eyes rapidly and tried to focus.

She turned to Denzel.

"Sorry about that," She said. "I was just panicking on my way over here and then when I finally saw you, the relief in me just took over my brain for a minute and I couldn't focus."

"What are you talking about?" Denzel asked. Gabrielle sighed.

"It's all over the news that someone was shooting over here. When I came that same day I saw caution tapes and the police and I had no idea if you were hurt or even worse!" Gabrielle exclaimed.

"You could have just called me," Denzel replied.

"I didn't think you would answer. And I just wanted to physically see you. I know it's dumb but-"

"It's not dumb," Denzel said. He could understand why she wanted to see him. And the fact that she cared so much was different for her. Denzel appreciated it, and it took his mind off wanting to strangle her for what she did.

"Was anyone hurt?" Gabrielle asked.

"My husband was shot," Charm supplied. Denzel gave Charm a look. She knew her mistake immediately. She was so used to calling Terrell her husband that the words just fell out of her mouth.

"Well we're separ-"

"He survived though," Denzel said cutting her off. Clearly he didn't want her to further explain herself. She'd already fucked up.

"Oh my god, I'm so sorry," Gabrielle gasped. "Just thinking about Denzel being hurt drove me crazy, I know you must feel the same."

"Um, it's sad yeah but he's alive and well that's all that matters." The three of them were silent for a moment.

"Oh and Charm I know how we first met wasn't quite pleasant. And what we've been through and said to each other well it wasn't very nice either. I'm trying to be a better woman and knowing that I know I have to apologize to you. Especially for disrupting your place of business. It wasn't right of me." Denzel titled his head to the side. Who was this woman?

"Who are you and what have you done with Gabby?" Denzel asked. Gabrielle smiled then laughed. The easiness of her laughter reminded him of their high school days. It was actually really refreshing to hear.

"That's very mature of you Gabrielle. Thanks for that. But I think out of us all, Denzel is the one that deserves your apology more than anything." Gabrielle looked at Denzel. He was looking her up and down as if he really thought she wasn't the same person he'd always known.

"I know that," Gabrielle said. "But that's something for me and him to handle in private. But I'm just real happy to see him alive and well right now." Charm felt worry seeping into her bones. She was a little confused as to how all of a sudden Gabrielle had this big change of heart. And what worried her more was that Denzel seemed complacent. He wasn't upset, but he wasn't happy either. He was just looking at her. Charm would pay to know what was running through his head.

"If you want Denzel me and you could I don't know, maybe just go to a lounge? Have drinks and talk?" Again Denzel was surprised. Gabrielle hated to go to lounges. She thought it was beneath her.

"I don't know what's going on with you right now Gabby, and even if you're sorry I just can't really accept it right now. I need time. What you did-that's not something I can get over easily." Gabrielle nodded.

"I knew that would be the case. And I'm not rushing you at all Denzel. But I just want you to know that despite my undesirable qualities, I will always and have always cared about you. But I won't press the issue anymore that it needs to be. We can talk another time." Denzel only nodded.

"But um, I actually want to talk to Charm. Woman to woman." Gabrielle looked right at Charm. She was beginning to see fire again but she didn't want to show it outright.

"I'll be in the basement," Denzel said raising his brows. He looked at both the women before walking off. Gabrielle waited until Denzel was completely out of earshot.

"Are you sure your husband is alright?" Gabrielle asked her.

"He's fine. Trust me."

"Now I know this may come off as a little rude. But hey we're women. Sometimes we can be catty. But I think I have a right to ask if you've been sleeping around with him. And I think you'll be woman enough to tell me the truth." Charm chuckled.

"Didn't Denzel break up with you?" Charm asked. "So why is it your right to know anything? And who says I have to tell you jack?"

"We were still dating when you came into the picture Charm. And then all of a sudden he ups and leaves me. I just want to know if you had something to do with that." Gabrielle advanced towards her but Charm didn't back down.

"Denzel didn't cheat on you Gabrielle. He's not that kind of man. I think you're the cause of the ending of your own relationship. Not me."

"Maybe you're right. And I think that you're not answering my original question because you are sleeping around with him now. And hey, you two are free to do what you please. But does your husband know that you're fucking around while he's laid up in a hospital?" Charm crossed her arms and didn't answer.

"I didn't think so," Gabrielle said. "Denzel, he's got a bomb ass dick don't he?" Even though Gabrielle was teasing Charm about this, she was pissed off another woman was able to experience what was hers.

"I can understand why would enjoy having sex with him. He satisfies you in more ways than you can ever imagine. I won't tell you to stop fucking him Charm cause like you said earlier it ain't my business anymore. But I will tell you not to fall for him."

"Excuse me?" Charm had to speak on that.

"Don't fall for him. Simple. He's going to break your heart."

"And how might I ask is he going to do that?"

"When he comes back to me Charm. That's how."

"And after killing his baby you think he'd ever want to be with you again?" Charm gasped. 'Damn you are crazier than you look."

"I know, we're at a bad place right now. But think about this Charm. We've been together for ten years. We've literally grown up together. And we've never taken a break from one another until now. I know Denzel deeper than you could even imagine. And once this all blows over and we actually make amends with each other, he's going to come straight home to me. Because I'm all he's ever known. You're just his fuck buddy Charm. And if you can't commit anything else towards him, then he's going to come back to the woman he knows he can get commitment out of. Sex between you and him means nothing. And in your heart I think you know that." Charm flashed back to what Denzel told her before they came to the gallery. That their sex wasn't as meaningful as he wanted it to be because they weren't exactly committing to each other.

"So I guess once you get it all out of your system and stop fucking him, you can go back to your husband and be the wife he needs and not the chick who's sprung on a man that doesn't belong to her."

The door to the basement opened. Gabrielle backed up immediately and plastered that smile on her face when she saw Denzel. Charm backed away before walking away completely.

"I'm gonna get going now," Gabrielle said. "I know you must have a ton of work to do Denzel."

"Um yeah," He replied giving her a look. She pointed at his canvas that had a half finished painting on it."

"It looks like it's going to be an amazing piece," She complimented. Denzel couldn't help but tilt his head to the side and look at the woman who he swore didn't give a damn about his artwork or that this was an actual job. Now she was complimenting it and being genuine about it? Denzel didn't know what to feel.

"Bye," She waved.

"Bye," Denzel whispered. Charm saw how Denzel watched Gabrielle leave. In that moment she was beginning to think that even if Gabrielle was a bitch the things she'd just said was completely true.

After a moment Denzel cleared his throat and looked away. His eyes found Charm. She was standing with her arms wrapped around herself, deep in thought.

"I'd love to know what the heck the two of you talked about," Denzel said.

"How does it make you feel to see her?" Charm asked.

"A little strange. She's never been that caring. I mean I know she cares about me, but she doesn't show it so openly. It was refreshing. She probably did it because she knew it would want to strangle her if she came up in here on her high horse."

"It looked to me as if you were interested in her again. I don't know you had this look on your face when you looked at her." Denzel shrugged.

"We've been together for ten years. I imagine that I'll always look at her a certain way. And I don't know, today she reminded me of the person I fell in love with in high school."

"So you want her back?" Charm asked.

"Whoa, wait a minute," Denzel said. "I told you how I felt about you. And if I feel a certain way about you then I can't possibly want her back. What in the hell did she say to you?"

"She wanted to know if we were having a sexual relationship."

"Figures. You should have asked her if she was having sex with anyone. I would have liked to know that."

"Why?" Charm asked. Denzel didn't want to tell her this but he wasn't going to start being dishonest when they'd barely even begun to have a relationship.

"I told you before that I took her virginity," Denzel said. "And I know she hasn't slept around while we were together. So if she still hasn't slept around then I've been the only man she's been sexual with."

"And...didn't you say that she took your virginity too?" Charm asked.

"Yeah she did. And in ten years I haven't cheated on her either. So I'm a year away from being 30 and I've only ever slept with one woman. Until of course there was you." Charm couldn't believe what he was saying. It was sort of amazing that he had that much commitment to allow himself never to sleep around on his girlfriend and to have given his body to one woman until they were broken up. But even if it was incredible Charm was hit with a fear that Gabrielle's words didn't have empty meanings. Denzel had really only known her and maybe once he got tired of fooling around with Charm, Gabrielle is exactly who he'd go back to.

"Charm," Denzel said trying to catch her attention. She pulled herself out of her thoughts and looked him.

"Hm?" She asked.

"What's on your mind?" he asked.

"Nothing," She replied trying to force herself to smile. "Anyways I think we should actually get to work." She nodded at him and walked off to get her canvas so she could continue what she was doing. Denzel was a little worried at what Gabrielle could have told her because Charm was in too deep a thought. The situation between all of them was kind of weird to begin with and he seriously didn't want anything to make it even more awkward. Even if he dated Gabrielle so long, he knew how he felt when he ended their relationship and he knew that the way he craved Charm was different. And he was going to work to make everything meaningful between them.

Chapter Nine

When Gabrielle left the gallery she went back to her car. She didn't realize Charm had a husband. And now that she had that information and idea was sparking in her head. Since she knew the shooting was on the news she went on the website to find the article about it. Charm hadn't told her his name so Gabrielle was hoping the article would tell her.

"Real estate agent Terrell Robinson huh?" Gabrielle smiled. The article detailed him being shot and treated at St Albans hospital. So with his name and knowing his location Gabrielle put her car in drive and headed in that direction. She didn't know outright what was her full plan but she needed to out Charm for the cheating wife that she was. Maybe if Charm had to deal with her husband more she would leave Gabrielle's man alone.

It took her about 20 minutes to get to the hospital. She hadn't put in her head anything she was going to tell Terrell yet but she'd cross that bridge when she got there.

"Hi, I'm here to see Terrell Robinson," Gabrielle told the receptionist. Since it was visiting hours she readily told Gabrielle the floor he was on and she was free to go. On the 5th floor, Gabrielle encountered another desk and she told the nurse who she was here to see.

"Okay give me a moment. Let me just make sure he's ready for a visitor." She smiled at Gabrielle and walked off.

"Terrell you have a visitor." Terrell looked up from his phone at the nurse who entered his room. Destiny jumped up.

"Visitor? Who?" She questioned.

"Someone named Gabrielle?" Terrell furrowed his brows. He was ready to tell the nurse he didn't know a Gabrielle but Destiny took charge. She didn't know who the hell was coming to visit Terrell but because it was a female, Destiny wasn't going to have her waltzing up in here until she explained her presence first. She already had to be dealing with Charm. She wasn't going to tolerate dealing with another woman.

Destiny followed the nurse out of the room. The woman standing down by the nurse's station was tall and ethereal. Her hair was pulled into a low ponytail. She wasn't that curvaceous, but she had a nice body shape that any man would want to hold onto.

"Can I help you?" Destiny asked, leaving the nurse behind and going up to the woman. She turned around and faced Destiny.

"If you can take me to see Terrell then yes you can help me," Gabrielle said.

"Well no I won't be taking you to see Terrell until I know who the hell you are." If this woman thought she could be the bitchiest then she would be in for a real surprise. Because Destiny was just as bitchy and bratty.

"So then you tell me who the hell you are," Gabrielle snapped. "I'm not just gonna confide in no random ass woman."

"I'm far from random girl. I'm Terrell's woman and the mother of his baby." Gabrielle stepped back and looked the woman up and down. What in the hell was going on?

"How can you be his woman if Charm is his wife?" Gabrielle asked. Destiny returned her look.

"You know Charm?" Destiny asked.

"Yes! And I came here to tell her husband that she's sleeping around on him with my man! But it looks like Terrell is doing his own sleeping around."

"Wait, Mr. Dark and Chocolate is your man?" Destiny laughed. Gabrielle crossed her arms. It was clear she was talking about Denzel.

"His name is Denzel," Gabrielle stated tartly. "And now I see Charm is messing around with him because she's trying to get back at Terrell for having you." Gabrielle stomped her foot.

"Now how am I gonna get rid of the bitch?!" She snapped to herself. Destiny saw then that Gabrielle was here because she was trying to get Charm out of her hair. But Destiny wanted to get rid of Charm that much too.

"My name is Destiny," Destiny told her. "I think we'll have a lot to talk about. We have something in common."

"Which is what?" Gabrielle asked.

"We both want Charm out of our hair."

"That's an understatement," Gabrielle huffed.

"Look, I'll be here with Terrell until visiting hours are over. Meet me tomorrow night at this place call Phat Cat. It's a lounge slash bar. We'll get drinks and we'll talk."

"What time?" Gabrielle asked.

"At ten."

"Okay fine, I'll be there," Gabrielle nodded. Both women looked each other up and down again. Gabrielle agreed to meet with her because she wanted to know things about Charm and Destiny would probably know that information. And if the both of them were trying to get rid of the same woman they could possibly succeed together. But Gabrielle didn't care to make a new friend. She just wanted her man.

"See you tomorrow," Destiny said. "And no matter what you want to do with Charm because she's sleeping with Mr. Dark and Chocolate, you're to stay away from Terrell. You're not on his level." Gabrielle chuckled and looked the woman up and down.

"You're the one that's gonna have a big belly in front of you in a couple months. Not me," Gabrielle laughed. "See if you'll be riding a dick with that." Destiny realized Gabrielle was good competition. They were both bitchy alike which meant they would both have crazy plans to get rid of Charm for good.

"You've got a lot to learn," Destiny said. "In this game Terrell values his baby more than my body. So like I said, you ain't on my level. See you tomorrow." Destiny looked Gabrielle up and down before turning away and walking off. She didn't even look back as she went back to Terrell's room.

"So who's Gabrielle?" Terrell asked.

"She knows Charm," Destiny answered. "Heard about the shooting and was coming to see if you were alright. I told her you were and she was satisfied with that and then she left. I figured you didn't want to be bothered by another woman right now."

"You're right. I can't deal with any more shit." Terrell shook his head. He'd been trolling Charm's Facebook page since that dude blew up on him and left with Charm. Terrell felt like a complete sucka at the moment. His phone was finally retrieved with the clothes that he was wearing that was torn off him when he was rushed to the operating room. So after Charm was gone and he got his phone back he was excited that he could text her and hope she would answer. Of course when she didn't reply to any of his messages he took to just trolling on her Facebook page. She was going to have to do a hell of a lot to get rid of him. As long as there was a way for him to save his marriage, Terrell was going to try anything. He was monitoring both her personal page and her company page. She didn't post anything on her personal page, but

Terrell found that she made a new post on the business page for her gallery advertising a new paint session she was hosting for the weekend. Terrell grunted in anger. He knew if he played to her love for art then he would get back in her good graces slowly. But he was trapped here, stuck in this hospital because he was having a hard time breathing.

"Look, I'm gonna get going soon," Destiny said. Terrell looked at her sharply.

"You're leaving me?" He questioned. "Visiting hours aren't over for a while!"

"I can't sit here all day with you Terrell! I have some business to take care of." Destiny came over to the bed and ran her hands along his face.

"Gonna miss me?" she asked. Terrell sighed.

"I'm just tired of being here. Charm won't talk to me, and now you're leaving. And I'm stuck here." Terrell grimaced at the pain in his chest.

"Let's get you some meds. You know that knocks you out. And once you open your eyes again I'll be back. Don't worry you'll be home soon." Destiny bent over and kissed him on the mouth. Terrell didn't know whether he should avert his head or just accept the action. He wasn't supposed to be doing anything like this with Destiny especially if he was trying to get his wife back. But it was a matter of knowing that Destiny was going to be in his life especially since she was the first woman to carry his seed. At just that thought he felt like he shouldn't turn away from her. So he didn't. He allowed her to kiss him, and when she deepened the kiss to add her tongue, Terrell accepted the kiss. He grabbed the back of her head and plunged his tongue into her mouth. This was the first kind of intimacy he'd experienced since the shooting. Strangely though he was still in pain, the kiss gave him something to think about other than his troubles with Charm and the fact that he was still cooped up in a hospital bed. He felt his shaft begin to harden as he tasted Destiny's lips. Now he could kind of remember why he fell into her temptation in the first place and succumbed to having sex with her when he knew he shouldn't have. Destiny reached down his gown and palmed his erection.

"Don't worry, when you finally get out of here I'll take care of you." Destiny bit his lips and finally moved away from him. Terrell licked his lips and closed his eyes. He couldn't believe he allowed her to get to him again. But how could anyone ask a man to resist? Terrell figured there was nothing wrong with it if for the time being Charm refused to be his wife. Once she stopped all her nonsense and came home, then Terrell's focus would be on her.

****

While Gabrielle had to wait until the next night to see Destiny, she had nothing to do. She went home and stared off into space thinking about Denzel. She'd been incredibly nice when it came to dealing with Charm but inside she saw multiple ways she could beat the mess out of her. And to think they were at the gallery alone just bonding and shit made Gabrielle extremely jealous. But she'd already showed up once. If she showed up twice what would be her luck that Denzel wouldn't snap at her? She huffed and rolled over on the bed. She just wanted her man back, that's all. But pushing him to be in her presence right now would make things worse. She hoped that Destiny could give her some useful information. But for the time being she was stuck in a rut not knowing what to do with her time. In her mind she wanted to go back to the gallery and just stay in her car and watch the place, but she didn't want to become that woman. So she stayed put and fought that urge. She went to go lay in bed and after a moment her eyes began to drift close. But Denzel was still in the forefront of her conscience and she smiled to herself as a dream of how Denzel use to treat her presented itself.

"You know you're so beautiful right?" Denzel asked her. Gabrielle turned in his hold and smiled at him. She felt her cheeks getting red as he gazed at her.

"I think I should know by now you tell me that every day," She said.

"Because I want to make sure you never forget it," He kissed her on the lips lightly.

"Denzel I'm scared," She sighed. "What if I am pregnant? We're graduating soon and we'll both have degrees and we want to start our careers. Can we even afford a baby?"

"We don't even really know if you're pregnant yet though Gabby."

"But what if I am?! Do you think we should abort?" Denzel gave her a sharp look. He sat up and pulled her with him.

"I want you to listen to me," Denzel said sternly. "And here me when I say this." He held her arms.

"I don't care what position we're in and what we have coming in our future. But if we lay down and make love, especially unprotected then we have to deal with whatever comes out of it. I love you Gabrielle and I wanna be with you. So in no circumstance are you to ever, ever think that I would want you to have an abortion. That will never ever be an option for us. I won't kill something we laid down and made."

"Are-are you sure?" She asked shakily.

"Of course Gabby. I mean, we're gonna get married someday aren't we?" He smiled at her.

"Not if you become a street painter with that degree of yours," She joked. Denzel sucked his teeth and pushed her back down on the bed.

"Don't play with me," He smiled. He began pulling down her pajama shorts.

"Denzel no!" She laughed trying to stop his hands. "We're panicking over me possibly being pregnant and you want to have sex right now?"

"I mean if you think about it if you're pregnant already then us having sex won't make a difference. And I guess I can wear a condom. But you're the one that hates condoms not me."

"I mean I hate the way they feel!" She protested. "But I'm scared." Denzel stopped trying to take her shorts off and leaned down to kiss her again. He rested his body over hers in a way that wouldn't put all his weight on her.

"Don't be scared Gabrielle. Whether you're pregnant or not, I'll be here for you. We've been together since senior year in high school and now look at us; about to graduate college. I ain't going nowhere girl. And if my baby is in your belly I'm only going to worship you more." Gabrielle wrapped her arms around his neck and kissed him deeply. They laid there in bed kissing but when he reached for her shorts again his body above her began to fade and slowly melt away like mist. Gabrielle struggled to keep him in her hold but he continued to dissipate. When he was completely gone from atop her, Gabrielle sat up quickly afraid of what was happening.

"Denzel?" She looked around the same dorm apartment they shared but saw no sign of him. A small squeal and cry caught her attention. Gabrielle nearly jumped ten feet out of the bed when she saw a small figure kneeling in the corner of the room. Gabrielle slowly went to the edge of the bed but she never got off.

"Hey," she called out softly. "What are you doing here?" she asked. The small figure sniffled and stopped crying.

"Why are you mad at me?" the voice that came from the figure was neither male nor female. Gabrielle was confused as to who the little person even was. With their backs turned to her she could see they were wearing a t-shirt that was too big for their body.

"What do you mean? I'm not mad," Gabrielle said.

"You want to send me away."

"No-no I haven't," Gabrielle was confused. "What are you talking about? And how did you get in here?"

"You-you brought me here," the child sniffled. "Don't you remember?"

"No I didn't bring you here. You've got it all wrong. So where's your parents?" The child turned around abruptly. Gabrielle fell out of the bed as the sight of the faceless child nearly stopped her heart. She picked herself up and pressed her back against the bed. Though the child had no face their skin was a chocolate, just like Denzel's. It was then that Gabrielle noticed the short spikes of locks falling from the child's head.

"No," Gabrielle gasped trying to get away. "Who are you?!"

"Don't you remember mommy?" The child tried to get closer to her. "Why don't you want me? Have I done something wrong? Is that why you got rid of me? Don't be mad at me please."

"Stop, stop it," Gabrielle cried covering her face so she couldn't see the child anymore.

"Mommy please take me back."

"No! Go away please leave me alone. I didn't mean it! I-I didn't mean it-" Gabrielle started to break down. She looked back up at the faceless child and held herself and just cried.

Gabrielle jumped out of her sleep, sweat dripping from her temples and on her chest. She looked around the dark room ready to see the faceless child but everything was different. She was in her own place in her own bed and not in her dorm apartment from college. Her chest heaved up and down as she tried to breathe. Through the dark she reached for her cell phone on the night table. Without hesitation she called the only person she ever reached out to when she had nightmares, or she just needed them.

"Gabby?" Denzel's deep voice was already giving her

comfort even though he didn't sound too pleased to talk to her.

"I'm sorry I called you Denzel I know you're still pissed at me, but-but I just had this horrible nightmare and I-I can't-"

"Calm down Gabrielle," He said softly. "Breathe. In. Out." Gabrielle took her time and did what he said. When she exhaled she could feel her heart slowing down.

"Okay," she said lowly. "But I'm still scared."

"Go on and turn on some lights Gabrielle." Gabrielle slowly got out of bed and reached for her lamp on her dresser.

"Can-can you come over?" she asked lowly. Denzel blew air out of his mouth.

"Gabrielle no. I told you earlier I would need some time. Don't try and force me into something that you know I'm not ready for."

"I know, but-"

"There is no but's. And I refrained my anger earlier because you were there apologizing to Charm but that bullshit apology shit won't work easy for me."

"Tell me how to fix it," Gabrielle sniffled.

"Fix it? Gabrielle, you killed my fucking baby. Unless you can go back in time there is no fixing it! Just-just leave me alone for now." With that said, Denzel hung up the phone. Gabrielle sat there feeling pathetic. Why did she have to go and get that abortion? Well, he wasn't even supposed to find out about it. It was her stupid emotions that let her blurt out the truth of what she'd done. She felt like a complete idiot now. She wished she could be in Denzel's arms right now, instead of just being home and staring at the walls thinking about that faceless child from her dreams. Gabrielle wondered what their baby would look like. With her fair skin and his chocolate one, no doubt they would have made a pretty baby.

"Stupid," Gabrielle said hitting her forehead. If she had just sat down and thought about it she would have realized that a baby would have made Denzel not only want her but actually marry her once they started a family. And with one bad decision she had screwed that up. Well now it was time for her to make things right. Denzel was going to be hers again.

Chapter Ten

Destiny walked into the bar at exactly ten o'clock the following night when she was to meet up with Gabrielle. She was wearing a tight red dress and her stilettos. She took what Gabrielle took to heart and wanted to dress up to show that she wasn't just no average side chick. But inside the bar, Destiny froze. Gabrielle was sitting at the long bar dressed extravagantly. Her short dress sparkled in the dark club getting her the attention of various men. Two were standing by her laughing and chatting with her. One of them kept motioning for the bartender to keep her glass filled with whatever alcoholic drink she was consuming. Destiny shook her head and continued towards the bar. She cleared her throat when she approached them. Gabrielle was just popping a cherry in her mouth.

"Oh Destiny! You're here," Gabrielle exclaimed. "Sorry gentlemen but my company is here. We've got business."

"Well then let me get your number so I can call you later," One of the guys said.

"She don't want your number cause she's gonna be calling me," The other guy argued. Destiny rolled her eyes.

"No one getting her number. Go away!" Destiny snapped at them. "Get out of here!" After sucking their teeth and muttering expletives, both of the men walked away. Destiny shook her head and sat in the empty stool next to Gabrielle.

"Can I get you something?" The bartender asked her.

"She'll have a pineapple juice with some seltzer," Gabrielle spoke for her. Destiny gave Gabrielle the side eye but then smiled to the bartender.

"Don't side eye me," Gabrielle said. "You the one that's pregnant. You look real hot though," Gabrielle complimented.

"You're pretty sexy yourself," Destiny said. "So that's my one good deed for the day. Complimenting your ass." Gabrielle just laughed and continued sipping on her drink.

"How much of that did you have?" Destiny asked.

"Not enough," Gabrielle scoffed. "But whatever. Tell me what's up with this Charm chick and why she's all over my man and not sticking with hers." Destiny rolled her eyes and sighed.

"Well Charm had a little woman problem. I guess something's wrong with her uterus or whatever but she can't carry kids. Her husband Terrell wanted to have a baby and Charm wasn't producing what he wanted so he hired me to do it."

"So how does that lead Charm to fucking Denzel?"

"She caught Terrell having sex with me and she went ballistic. Said she was calling off their marriage and she didn't want to be with him anymore. I have no idea where she met this Denzel or how long she knew him for. But I assume after she left Terrell that's who she went to." Gabrielle threw her drink back not bothering to sip anymore.

"Denzel works for her at her gallery. And what? It's been like three months or something and now they're all lovey dovey and shit? I can't believe it. And for him to sleep with her that easy, like what the hell? I don't get it."

"Yeah well it happened. Just get over it. The problem now that we both seem to have is that Charm's invading our relationships and she's not wanted. You want Denzel and I want to keep Terrell."

"But if she left Terrell to begin with why are you even concerned about it? She doesn't want him, she's coming after Denzel."

"Well because Terrell is convinced he wants his wife back. I just need to work on him more to make him forget her, but I'm afraid that she's going to come to her senses or something and come running back to Terrell to take him back. And if you get Denzel back then that's going to be a problem for me," Destiny said.

"Then that stands to question why you're even trying to help me," Gabrielle inquired.

"Because if the both of us don't do something then she'll never be out of the picture for good. And I'm pretty sure Denzel won't just let Charm walk away without trying to get her back. So she needs to go. And if she's gone we'll both be happy."

"So then what you suggest?" Gabrielle asked. "Because the way I see it, she's pretty invested in Denzel right now. And in fact, Denzel is invested in her like you said. So what do we do huh? Can't kidnap her and fling her off the side of a mountain or some shit." Destiny gave Gabrielle a look.

"No we can't kidnap her or throw her off a mountain psycho," Destiny scoffed. "I mean we could do something less dramatic like maybe I don't know, poisoning her. But without a doubt, you, me, and maybe even Terrell will all be suspects. And it's not like we can pin her murder on anyone else."

"We can make it look like an accident," Gabrielle suggested. Again Destiny had to wonder if Gabrielle had all her marbles. Or maybe she was down to do anything just to get her man back.

"As much as I'd like to get rid of her that way, and as evil as I can be, I'm not tryna kill anyone. So try again," Destiny scolded.

"It's almost like we can't get rid of her without doing something illegal! So what else do you suggest?"

"First off tell me why the hell Denzel left you and went with Charm in the first place?" Destiny asked. "I need to know the whole story." Gabrielle rolled her eyes.

"We've been together since we were 18 and in high school. And after all that time he refuses to marry me. And he doesn't want to marry me because I demand him to get a real job and not play around in his little paint like he does all day. He doesn't want that serious commitment and we fell out because of it. But now even if I try to talk to him he won't give me the time of day."

"Why not?"

"I got an abortion without telling him," Gabrielle admitted. Destiny wasn't shocked. A woman like Gabrielle was clearly vain.

"So even if you got rid of Charm how in the hell do you think he's even gonna want you after that?"

"I don't know! But I want my man back. He's the only one in the world for me. And don't try to tell me otherwise!" Destiny knew there was no point in actually telling her to give up on Denzel.

"It looks like the only answer besides getting rid of Charm is giving him back what you took from him," Destiny suggested.

"How?! I just told you he won't even speak more than a couple words to me, much less lay down with my ass and fuck me!"

"Calm down!" Destiny snapped. "You wanna know how I got pregnant?" Gabrielle crossed her arms and listened.

"I saw the way Terrell would look at me. And the way he treated me it was clear he was interested. But he was on that 'I'm not cheating on my wife' bullshit. Which doesn't even matter now because he still ended up fucking me. But the way I got pregnant was all because the power of a drug. Gave it to him in his drink, he was incoherent and dazed. I went to work then, changed into a cute little outfit and kissed and touched him. When he was hard enough I got on top and rode him until he came inside me. Now thinking about it, it was pretty clever on my part." Gabrielle sat there with her mouth open. After a moment she blinked and called for the bartender. She had to order another drink. Once she got her martini she sipped it before eating her cherry.

"Now that I've digested all that information," Gabrielle said. "Are you telling me you basically raped him? And then told him you were pregnant a month later and he was just okay with it?"

"That's the thing," Destiny said. "We were drinking when I slipped him the drug, so when I told him I was pregnant I told him it was drunk sex. He didn't remember but he knew he was drinking and that's all it took. Plus, he was finally presented with the baby he always wanted. So no doubt he was going to accept it. And even if Charm left him I'm always going to have a place in his life. That's what you need to do with Denzel. For the right price I'll get you both the fertility drugs and the date rape." Gabrielle shook her head.

"Denzel doesn't drink alcohol," Gabrielle pouted. "No way I'm going to be able to get him to drink so I can drug him."

"Doesn't drink? What kind of man do you got?" Destiny teased.

"Shut up," Gabrielle snapped slapping Destiny on the arm.

"There's other ways to drug him. You just gotta give me time to get the right drugs. And if you're serious about this, you need to get on fertility medication to. That way it won't take much for you to get pregnant." Gabrielle crossed her arms.

"I don't know it sounds good and all but is it something I can really pull off?"

"Honestly that's up to you," Destiny said. "It's all about how bad you want your man. Me? I'm tired of living the low life. I want to have the finer things in life, plus a fine man. I didn't originally come in with the idea of taking Terrell from Charm but that's the way shit panned out. And now that I know Terrell wants me I won't back off. That's just what it boils down to for me. So you gonna start playing dirty or you gonna let another woman take your man?" Gabrielle just looked at her. She knew Destiny was right.

"You may not be able to get to Denzel as fast as you want to, but if you can get close to Charm then you need to start getting under her skin. But do it in a way where if she lashes out at you, she's gonna look like the crazy one. If she starts acting out, Denzel might start drifting away from her. Think about that. And maybe you should stop thinking about yourself and sacrifice your body to give that man something you took away from him." Gabrielle leaned back surprised that Destiny was saying that kind of thing to her. Even though Destiny was pregnant she didn't come off as the type that thought about anyone else but herself.

"That sounds rich coming from someone like you," Gabrielle said tartly.

"I mean I'm just saying. But if I gotta give my body up for 9 months to get the money, and the man. Then it is what it is," Destiny said.

"It ain't just 9 months Destiny. You gotta raise that thing too." Destiny waved her off.

"Terrell will be a great dad. That's what he's there for." Destiny sighed. "Listen, think about what I said. I'm gonna get you those drugs and just make sure you have payment for it. Take my number so we can talk the next time."

"Why don't you just stay for a little bit with me?" Gabrielle asked. Destiny thought for a moment. It wasn't like she had anything to go home to. If Terrell wasn't in the hospital it would be different but since he was Destiny figured it made no sense to go home to be alone.

"Alright, I'll chill with you, but I think we should go somewhere else. I can't fucking drink and it's depressing," Destiny pouted.

"Oh you ain't said nothing but a word. Let's hit the casino. I know a couple people, and the men there will love two hot bitches showing them some attention."

"The casino huh?" Destiny asked.

"And don't worry about losing money. If we talk to the right guy the right way, they'll be more than willing to play a couple games for us. Let's go." Gabrielle threw back the last of her drink and slid down the stool.

"And as you saw earlier, I know how to get the attention of a man," She winked. Gabrielle waved to the two men she was entertaining earlier.

"Let's go." Destiny shrugged her shoulders and followed Gabrielle out of the bar. She was in no place to judge another woman especially one that was probably more like her than she cared to admit, so Destiny kept her mouth shut. In the end at least she could have a good time for now. She was just a little pissed she couldn't even have a drink.

"Oh and by the way, the casino has some amazing red wine. It's not as good as a margarita but it'll give you a little buzz. Trust me."

"That's better than nothing," Destiny said. "I'm all for it." Even though they knew they weren't going to be best friends, they did have a common goal and for now it benefitted them. Besides wanting Charm out of the picture, for right now the both of them had another thing in common. And that was being alone.

Chapter Eleven

Charm watched as Denzel spoke harshly on the phone. He'd stepped to the side to take the phone call and immediately Charm had a feeling she knew who it was. It was a little past 8pm and they'd been at the gallery all night painting. Jason and Brianna and joined them, and it was like old times again with the four of them joking around and working. When Denzel left the group to take the call, Charm was a little bit worried. Since Gabrielle left earlier she couldn't stop thinking about what she said. Charm just had a feeling that Gabrielle wasn't going to let anything go easily.

"Who was that?" Brianna asked Denzel when he came back to his easel and sat on a stool.

"Gabby," He answered.

"Figures," Brianna scoffed. "I still wanna know what the hell she did to you. I knew the breakup was inevitable but you never gave me details. Next thing I know, I'm walking in on the two of you humping like gorillas." Jason snickered where he was sitting on a beanbag and looking at his IPad.

"I can't believe I missed a chance to see Denzel's chocolate ass," Jason muttered

"Stop it," Denzel snapped at him. At this point Jason knew Denzel hated when he said things like that, but he couldn't help messing around with the man.

"Stop messing with him," Charm chuckled.

"Oh look. Coming to his rescue," Brianna teased. "That's cute."

"Hush up," Denzel told her. Charm sighed and put her paintbrush down. It was by no means late, and in fact she's worked later than this before but right now she was feeling tired.

"I don't know about ya'll, but I think I'm done for the night," She sighed. She left from in front of her canvas and plopped down on a beanbag. She closed her eyes and took several deep breaths before opening them again.

"You okay?" Denzel asked her.

"Just a little tired. Which is weird because I've stayed up past this before."

"Well with all the stuff that's been happening you're

probably just stressed out," Jason said. "Not to mention you got hauled in by the cops too."

"I still can't believe it," Charm rubbed her eyes. "I was temporarily distracted by all of that, but guess it's still affected me. You wouldn't believe the way Terrell was speaking to me earlier, Jase."

"Temporarily distracted by what?" Jason asked. He didn't miss when Charm and Denzel looked at each other.

"And I can probably guess how he was speaking. I can't believe he even has the audacity to say certain shit when he has a pregnant mistress. Anything he says is invalid when it comes to me. You should feel the same."

"Denzel handled him for me so it did make me feel a lot better. If not for him I don't know that I wouldn't still be crying my eyes out."

"So that's what had you distracted?" Jason asked.

"Well there was other things," Charm said. When she looked at Denzel again, he was already gazing at her. Denzel realized she was talking about the sex they'd been having. Yes, it was a distraction for the both of them but Denzel wanted it to be more than that. And in that he knew he just had to do more for her.

"Honestly Charm, you're an amazing ass woman, but you need to grow some balls. I know you play that wife role really well, but the man disrespected you. Drop all that shit and cuss his ass out. All this crying and whatnot is just making him feel like he's won something. And he hasn't," Brianna said.

"I know Brianna. And eventually I really need to get my act together." Charm shook her head and rubbed her eyes. "I'm ready to get in bed."

"You want to come back to my place? Or go with your knight in shining armor over there?' Jason asked her. Charm chuckled.

"Well my suitcase is at your place. And I'm running out of things to wear at Denzel's loft. I don't want to keep invading his space either." Charm looked at Denzel ready for him to tell her that he disagreed. He smiled at her but didn't outright tell her she was talking nonsense.

"It's all up to you Charm," Denzel said. "Even though you promised me something earlier you do look exhausted. But it's your choice where you stay for the night."

"You also have a say in it Denzel. It's your place."

"I know I'm cool with it. Then it just depends on what you want doesn't it?" Thinking about being cuddled up next to him took over her brain not allowing her to think of any other possibility.

"Can we stop by your place Jason so I can pick up some stuff? Then I'd like to cuddle under Denzel's fluffy sheets and get lost for the night in some deep sleep."

"That sounds like a good night. Even I'm jealous," Jason said. Charm shook her head when Denzel made a face.

"Now wait a minute," Brianna spoke up. "I'm all for the two of you hooking up, I can see how ya'll are feeling each other. But I told you Charm I don't want you stringing Denzel along, but I also don't think you two should be moving too fast either. So if you're really leaving your husband, where are you going to be living? I don't think you should be moving in with each other at all."

"Whoa," Charm said. "No one is talking about moving in. I can sleep at Jason's that's fine as well. And I'm not gonna get a new place until after the divorce. So right now my stuff is at Jason's but I was thinking about buying a blow up bed and just sleeping here. I did pay for the place so it's mine and not Terrell's. I'm going to have all my mail forwarded to the gallery, and that's that."

"You can't sleep here," Brianna exclaimed. "And I'm not tryna be a bitch but-"

"Don't worry about it," Charm said "I get it."

"Whether we're moving too fast or not Charm, I won't allow you to sleep here all alone. You can stay at my place whenever you want to," Denzel spoke up.

"And you know I won't let you sleep here either," Jason said. "So you're talking a whole bunch of shit." Charm looked at her best friend and smiled.

"Thanks Jase," She smiled.

"Alright," Denzel said. "I think I should take you to get some sleep,"

"If that's alright with you Brianna," Charm said as she stood. Brianna rolled her eyes and smirked.

"Bitch," She snickered.

"You started it," Charm laughed. Jason stood as well, putting his IPad up.

"Y'all are both bitches, how about that?" Jason said. "And come on, you guys gotta follow me to my place before you can get some rest Charm. So let's move it."

Everyone began packing up their things to get ready to leave the gallery. Brianna kept giving him a look as they packed up. Though she was hovering again, Denzel knew she did have a point. Ever since he saw Charm there was just something in him that triggered and he was smitten over her. Then with just one kiss everything erupted and Denzel couldn't help himself. Once the both of them were consenting for the right reasons, it all just happened fast. But that didn't mean that he didn't need to think about the moves he was making with her. The sex was incredible but they needed more than that.

"Lemme talk to you for a second," Denzel said to Brianna. Everyone turned to look at him when he said that which he kind of expected it. But thankfully Brianna walked towards the office with him without complaint.

"Don't scold me alright, you know I'm just trying to look out for you."

"No, no I get it. I'm not upset. And you are right anyways. I don't wanna move fast with her, but I need to give her much more than what I've been giving her."

"Which is just sex right?"

"Well I do give her comfort," Denzel countered.

"Look," Brianna started. "You're an amazing man. You don't really have to do much to get Charm to feel you. In fact, she's already feeling you hard. You two just need to make sure that you're not just lusting after each other. The both of you are in a delicate position."

"How so?"

"The both of you are fresh out of long term relationships. Which means that the both of you don't need to jump into anything too serious too quickly. Charm just wants someone that she can trust, and you need someone that can show you the affection Gabrielle didn't. I think Charm is that person for you. So just for a minute, stop feeling with your ding a ling, and feel with your heart." Denzel smiled. He appreciated her words and they did make sense. Charm had a lot of healing to do when it came to Terrell. And Denzel wasn't going to help her by just dicking her down. The both of them needed more than that. Even if it did feel incredible.

"I need you to do me a favor," Denzel said. "You down?"

"You know you don't gotta ask," Brianna said clapping

hands with him.

"I'll text you details tonight. I'll text Jason too. Maybe there's one thing he can help with."

"Gotcha. Get a move on. And remember, what I said about your ding a ling," She said.

"What about his ding a ling?" Charm asked. Brianna didn't know Charm was close enough to hear that bit.

"Nothing," Brianna laughed. Denzel smiled and took Charm's hand.

"Come on, we're leaving."

Brianna went her separate way in her own care after bidding everyone goodnight while Charm and Denzel followed Jason to his apartment. They didn't really speak during the car ride but they held hands. Denzel noticed that Charm kept yawning and he could tell she was truly tired. The enormity of the actual situation must have been weighing on her no matter if she didn't talk about it or deal with it.

They continued holding hands until they pulled up to Jason's place. Denzel was ready to follow her but she stopped him.

"It's okay I'll be right out," Charm said. "I'll only grab a couple of things I don't want to crowd your place."

"Don't be foolish. But get what you need." Charm kissed his cheek before she left the car. She hadn't packed all her things up from her home, but she had enough at Jason's house to last her for a while. Eventually however she would have to go to what was her home and start packing her things up. Not only the rest of her clothes, but all her other personal items. Just thinking about a divorce gave her a headache. It was the splitting things in half and who got what, and who was supposed to pay who, but Charm didn't want to deal with all of that. And she didn't want to become one of those ex-wives dependent on money for their ex-husbands. Things would definitely be different but Charm would be able to manage.

"See you later," Jason hugged her tightly after she grabbed some stuff.

"I know I'm all over the place but I promise I'll get my shit together. Right now, I just enjoy spending time with him."

"Girl you do not have to explain yourself. Because I know exactly what you must be feeling. I just want you to find a peace of mind. But anyone can have sex with someone Charm. But it's actually allowing yourself to feel more than that with him that will help heal your broken heart. And I don't care how good he lays it down Charm. Your heart is still broken. Especially after you've given ten years to one man." Charm sighed.

"I know. I guess I just don't want to say anything because I don't want it to seem as if I'm hung up on Terrell. And I'm not."

"Even if you are, it's okay Charm. Because you need the time to let yourself overcome it. But I'm glad Denzel is here for you. No doubt if you just had me you'd still be a huge mess, no matter how I try to help."

"Trust me, there's a lot I wouldn't be able to do without you Jase. Know that." Charm hugged him one more time before kissing him on the cheek and bidding him good night.

Back in Denzel's car, she rested back and resumed holding his hand. Her car was still parked by his place, and because she was always with him, she didn't have to drive anywhere. He was always willing to take her anywhere. It felt a little new to her because she and Terrell hardly ever drove in the same car anymore. In fact they didn't do things together at all! So being in Denzel's car, holding his hand felt good. And when he moved his hand to her thigh and began rubbing it slowly, Charm couldn't help but moan low in her throat and relax even deeper. And there was nothing sexual about the way he was touching her in that moment, and Charm appreciated that more than she thought she ever would. Before she knew it, she was asleep in the quiet and cozy drive back to his loft.

Denzel realized that when he pulled up to his loft and parked, Charm didn't move. He'd had his hand on her thigh but he was mostly concentrating on the road so he hadn't looked over at her until he pulled over. And when he looked, she was fast asleep with her head tilted to the side. Denzel moved her short hair from her face and looked at her sleeping. She was so damned beautiful, he was just still full of shock at the fact that he was getting this opportunity to spend time with her.

Getting out of the car, he grabbed her bag of clothes, then went around her side to get her out of the car. He slung her bag over his shoulder, then carefully cradled her in her arms and got her out of the car. Slamming the door shut with his foot, he pressed the lock button on the key fob and carried her towards the loft. Luckily he could take the elevator right up to his loft and it didn't require him to compromise the way he was holding Charm. Inside his place he went straight to the bedroom so he could set her down on the bed. She didn't wake so after putting her bag down, he began undressing her. But when he reached for her hips to pull her pants down, she lifted her hips and moaned. Denzel flipped his eyes up to see her looking at him.

"You're too tired for that," He smiled. "Cut it out." Charm stretched and moaned some more. She wiggled her hips and Denzel kept pulling her pants down. She lifted her legs in the air and crossed them, making her lady lips pucker underneath her panties. He ran his fingertip along her slit and watched as her body shivered.

"Why do you do this to me?" Denzel asked, backing off. He was so hard he could already feel his balls clenching with aching need to release.

"Just because I'm tired doesn't mean I'm not still horny," She said lowly. "And I was in a deep sleep until I felt those hands of yours on me like that."

"Go take ya hot ass in the shower," Denzel ordered. "Bet you fall right asleep after that." Charm lifted her arms.

"Undress me," She begged with a pouty look.

"Such a baby," Denzel teased as he continued undressing her. He figured her motive for that was getting him hot to the point where he couldn't resist her, but for the moment Denzel kept control of himself. When she was naked, he pinched her nipple.

"Go on, so I can go after you," he said. She huffed but eventually got out of the bed and headed towards the bathroom. While she showered, Denzel unpacked her small bag and put it in the empty drawer of his dresser so she had a place to keep everything. She had some clothes folded on his small couch, but Denzel figured she wouldn't mind having a drawer. It wasn't like that meant she was moving in either. She just deserved to have her clothes in one spot.

"You need anything to eat baby girl?" Denzel asked poking his head into the bathroom.

"No, I'm fine," She responded. Denzel wasn't hungry himself so if she wasn't hungry he didn't have to prepare any food. He went back into the bedroom and waited until she was done so he could take his shower.

Like the little tease she was, she came out of the bathroom with the towel barely wrapped around her body. Denzel only gave her a glance before beginning to strip. He noticed that Charm loved to tease. But he didn't mind going tit for tat with her. And indeed when he turned around, she was the one staring at his naked body. He smirked and walked out of the room and headed for the bathroom to take his shower. He expected her to be fast asleep again by the time he returned but instead she was resting back against his pillows with her large sketch book in her lap. But instead of the clothes they'd just drove to get from Jason's house, she was wearing one of his t-shirts. When he entered the room, her eyes popped up to look at him. He noticed that she didn't stop looking at him even as her hand kept working. She bit her lip as Denzel dried off his shaft.

"Take a picture," He teased her. She flipped the sketchbook over and showed him the rough draft of what was looking like a drawing of him.

"Figures," He scoffed. "But put some clothes on me. Don't leave me naked. Someone might see it." He noticed immediately the prominent lines of his manhood in the drawing. And Charm was a very gifted artist, so it looked incredibly like the real thing.

"Naked drawings are always so pure," She said. That was true enough, but that didn't mean he wanted a naked drawing of himself being created. Someone undesirable might get ahold of it.

"Still don't mean I want you to have one of me."

"Oh please. Don't nobody wanna see your ass naked. So relax," She chuckled. Denzel made a face as he pulled on his boxer briefs and joined her in bed.

"I take my nakedness very serious," He said lying next to her. She cuddled next to him and rested her head against his shoulder and chest. He looked on as she continued to draw. Denzel was amazed at how incredible she was at drawing. It almost baffled him and he almost felt talentless when he watched her draw. Such raw talent shouldn't exist in one human being.

"You know you shouldn't waste your talent drawing my naked body," Denzel suggested.

"I think your naked body is worth drawing. At least I think so." She began adding detail to his manhood and the way she depicted it made Denzel look at her. She was too into it. And he had to wonder what was fueling it. Not like she was actually looking at it in the moment.

"Are you doing that from memory?" Denzel quizzed. "Cause I don't know if that's creepy or I should be flattered." Charm elbowed him and laughed.

"Yes I'm doing it from memory. And your ass should be

flattered that I know what it looks like without even seeing it. You've fucked me enough for me to know what it looks like from memory."

"But that's the thing Charm. When we're having sex you're not looking at my penis because that's what I'm using to be inside you."

"Then let's just say I'm using my muscle memory to draw," She winked up at him.

"You are something else," He smiled.

"But there's just this small part that I can't remember what it looks or feels like," She said lowly. Denzel looked to where she was tapping her pencil.

"I feel like there's a vein right there connecting to your base, but I'm not sure." She put the book down and sat up fully so she could turn and look at him. Denzel didn't know what she was playing at, but he saw that lusty gaze in her eyes.

"I thought you were tired," he whispered to her.

"I am." She breathed. "But I can't go to sleep until I've gotten my lullaby." She reached for the night table and cut of the lamp, bathing the room in darkness. Denzel stayed where he was until he felt her legs coming across his hips as she straddled him. She still had on her t-shirt but the heat he felt emanating from between her legs was too intense for her to be wearing underwear. Right away, Denzel was hardening again. And to think, he couldn't see her, she was still wearing a t-shirt, and at just the feel of her heat he was hard and ready to go.

"I need to feel your whole dick to finish my drawing," She whispered in his ear. Denzel knew she didn't but he was going to play her game simply because he couldn't be teased anymore. So he pulled down the front of his underwear and settled deeper into the bed. He let her take complete control. She rose up and guided herself on top of his shaft. All he did was hold her at the hips and guide her down. She let out a strained moan and stopped halfway.

"All the way," He coaxed.

"It's too fucking thick," She groaned. She was hot and slick and even if she felt a slight pain she was wet enough to take him completely.

"I know baby but you can take it. Come on, I wanna be deep inside you." He began pulling her hips down. Though she was gritting her teeth, she allowed herself to keep sliding down on his thick erection. When she reached his base, she gasped out. His tip was damn near poking at her intestines. Denzel seriously made it easy for her to say he was all in her guts.

"I'm waiting on you," Denzel said slapping her ass. "You wouldn't stop until you got on it. Now you on it." Charm braced herself on his chest and began moving back and forth, riding him slowly.

"Damn," he gritted as her muscles gripped him with her motions. The stark difference between Charm and Gabby was that Gabby fucked like she was a damn porn star. He figured after years of being with the same person you just had to spice shit up. He always enjoyed sex with Gabby, but now with Charm everything was so much more real. Like the way she rode him. it was slow but it still fulfilled a purpose. And she moaned when it was necessary. Gabrielle moaned about 100 percent of the time and Denzel knew damn well that even his dick didn't feel that good. The realness of Charm's moan's made him harder than he realized.

"You okay?" He asked her, kissing her neck and chin.

"Yes," She breathed, starting to pick up her pace. "Fuck!" She gritted. Denzel took her expletive as one that meant she was coming. And he didn't need her words to know that. He could feel her creaming on him without even having to look. Denzel grabbed a handful of both her ass cheeks and matched her pace, helping her rid him harder. He was trying to give her the control and not thrust upwards but it was hard to resist. Her body went still in his arms as her muscles clenched him in a tight hold.

"Oh shit," Denzel hissed throwing his head back. With her frozen in place Denzel had to begin thrusting upwards before his own orgasm began to recede. As if snapping out of her trance, Charm began grinding on his shaft.

"Come baby," She moaned. Denzel let her ass cheeks go as he body began to buck. She rose up and began only riding his tip.

"I'm coming Charm," He bit out. She quickly hopped off his shaft as his release began spurting out of him. She held his base and continued stroking him as he came completely. She squeezed his tip to get a shiver out of him.

"Fuck," He sighed. "Your shit feels too fucking good." He shook his head. Charm smiled at him as she fell back onto the bed. Just like he figured, when he looked down at his shaft, it was filled with cream from her orgasm. His eyes had adjusted to the dark enough to be able to see.

"Now I know what to draw," She said exhaustedly, pointing at his manhood.

"Well you ought to know now," Denzel scolded. He got out of bed so he could get a wash cloth and wipe her down. While in the bathroom he wiped off his stomach and wiped down his shaft cleaning it from all the cream she left behind. By the time he returned from the bathroom, Charm was literally knocked out, drawing snores in the middle of the bed.

"Seriously?!" He laughed. She only waved him off but never opened her eyes. Denzel spread her legs and cleaned her thoroughly. He fixed her on the bed and turned her back to the top of the bed. He pulled his underwear up and got in the bed next to her. He couldn't help but spoon her after what they'd just done.

"I want our sex to be meaningful too," she whispered to him. "And even if we can't move too fast, I love the time we do spend together and I will be looking forward to anything else that we do together." Denzel kissed her on the cheek.

"Sleep baby girl." He appreciated what she said, and with Brianna helping him he was going to make sure that they explored more with each other. It wasn't enough just to learn her body sexually. He wanted to learn so much more because down the line, he didn't want there to be any question as to why the two of them shouldn't be together.

Chapter Twelve

Denzel wanted to prove to Charm that he wanted her around for much more than just sex. Or well he did prove to her that he wanted more from her because of the way he treated her, but there was still much more for him to give. So with Brianna's help, he was ready to set up something nice for her. But in the meanwhile he was trying to refrain from having sex with her so much. That didn't seem like a problem since the next morning when they awoke, and a couple days later, Charm didn't seem like herself. The time she usually took to paint, she was using to sleep. After the third day of the same routine, Denzel was deeply concerned. She convinced him that she was fine but it was just unusual.

"Baby girl, I made some food," Denzel said going into his bedroom. Again, Charm was sleeping in bed. This was her third nap for the day. And it's been like that for the past couple days.

"Okay," she groaned. "I'm not really hungry though." Denzel went over to the bed and sat next to her. She turned over on her back so she could look at him.

"You worry me," He said to her.

"I'm just not hungry Denzel. I wanna just sleep."

"But you been sleeping all day Charm, and you haven't eaten all day." He looked down at her body. She wasn't losing as weight, not to him but not eating was a big concern. That's how she was when she initially left Terrell. He didn't want to have her retreating back into those emotions.

"I don't know I just feel weak."

"Want to go to a doctor?" Denzel asked.

"No. maybe I just need some vitamins." Denzel rubbed her thigh.

"Okay I'll get you some. I don't like seeing you like this." Charm smiled weakly. She wasn't sure what was up with her but she'd been feeling like no matter how much she slept she was just still tired. Not to mention she didn't want to eat anything.

"I hope this has nothing to do with Terrell." Denzel said. Charm gave him a look. She hadn't been thinking about Terrell a lot at all since she was sleeping in Denzel's arms for a couple days straight. With Denzel, she didn't have time to obsess over Terrell.

Instead of answering Denzel though she just sucked her teeth and turned away from him.

"What's that now? You upset at something?"

"You, for asking me dumb questions," She said.

"Don't get crazy with me," Denzel warned her. He'd barely experienced her attitude but in the moment he kind of didn't mind her being snappy. It showed that no one was ever perfect. And not all relationships was going to be without argument.

"Not like you gonna do anything about it. You haven't touched me in how many days now?" Denzel's eyes went wide. He turned Charm back over to make her look at him.

"You can barely keep your eyes open and you want me to try and fuck you?" He asked. "You think I'm that inconsiderate?" She pouted, pushing out her bottom lip. Denzel rolled his eyes at her cuteness. He could see that she was going to be hard to argue with.

"Just because I'm tired doesn't mean I'm not horny," She said. "Even now. I'm wet as fuck and you just been ignoring me." Denzel stood from the bed and shook his head.

"You're being hella unreasonable." She crossed her arms and pouted deeper. "Stop it," He sighed.

"No," She pouted. Denzel rubbed his eyes.

"When you get your energy back Charm, I'm all yours. Trust me. I just want you to be healthy." She sighed and rolled over.

"I guess so." Denzel didn't want to just leave her like that so he got in bed next to her, and cuddled with her.

"I'll never ignore your needs baby girl," He said. She nodded and rubbed her head into the crook of his neck. Again, within five minutes she was sleeping again. Vitamins hopefully would do the trick.

Thankfully, after another two days with taking vitamins, Charm actually started getting her energy back. She was active, and even her skin was bright. Denzel was relieved to see her back to normal, and that meant that he could move forward with the plans he had for her. The hardest thing to do was to resist her flesh. He wanted so bad to be inside her, rocking her to pleasure, but for what he had planned for her he wanted to resist having sex with her yet again. But when you had a woman like Charm around you all the time, it was easier said than done. With Gabby, he had his needs taken care of when he needed them taken care of. But if he went a week without fucking her he wouldn't get into a mood. He'd only just started making love to Charm, and not having sex with her for almost a week was driving him and his balls crazy. He was hard twenty-four seven had he could feel the hulk in his trying to emerge. Lack of sex never made him angry. But there was just something about not having Charm that triggered his anger. All because he was planning that special day and night for her, he was getting himself riled up. But he just had one more night to wait it out. And then he would have her all to himself.

****

"Rise and shine slut!" Charm jumped up at the sound of Brianna's high pitched voice. She looked around the room quickly to see it was only her and Brianna. Charm pushed down her t-shirt realizing it had rose up during her sleep.

"Damn you psycho!" Charm snapped at her. "And don't you see I'm not completely dressed?"

"Yes actually I can see that. Though I didn't take you for a manicured public hair type of girl. I always thought you'd be more of a bald type of chick." Charm gasped and closed her legs tighter and pulled the covers over herself.

"I can't believe you," Charm gasped. "That you'd just stand here gazing at my damn vagina and be okay with it!"

"I'm an artist Charm. You'd have to be real disgusting for nudity to affect me. Now up and at 'em. We got things to do."

"Where's Denzel?" Charm asked.

"He went to get a shape up. He asked me to come over and hang out. Keep you company and shit. And I thought, aye what a good idea. It's always me and Jason because you and Denzel is off being lovebirds. And since I just got an eyeful of your lady parts I think I am entitled to spending a day with you." Charm shook her head.

"You can always ask me to hang out Brianna," Charm said. "I would love it. But this is the second time you caught me in a precarious position and I don't know what to say about it."

"Not my fault Denzel gave me a key. Are you getting up or what?"

"I'm getting up, I'm getting up," Charm sighed. Indeed when she looked next to her, the space that Denzel occupied was made up neatly and he was gone. Was Charm that knocked out that she didn't even feel when he got up to leave?

Charm headed straight for the bathroom leaving Brianna in the room. She didn't know what they were about to do, but she brushed her teeth and hopped in the shower to completely wash up. Back in the bedroom Brianna was flipping through Charm's sketchbook.

"Girl you're so talented," Brianna said. "And this is just sketches. I can't even believe how amazing this is. I don't think I'll ever be this good."

"Don't say that," Charm said. "You're real good too you know and I-"

"Whoa!" Brianna shouted. Charm looked over to see she was staring at the sketch of the naked Denzel that Charm had been working on. Charm lunged for the sketchbook and ripped it out of Brianna's hand. She snapped the book closed.

"That wasn't for you to see!" Charm snapped. "That's mine!" Brianna held her hands up.

"You could have warned me as I was flipping through the damn pages! I swear if I have to see Denzel's dick one more time," Brianna shook her head. Charm was holding the sketchbook against her chest protectively.

"Did you see everything?" Charm asked lowly.

"Well it's hard to miss the giant dick as soon as you look at it," Brianna scoffed. Brianna noticed immediately the look on Charm's face and the way she grabbed after the book in the first place.

"I'm still just his best friend Charm," Brianna said.

"But you're still a woman," Charm replied.

"I promise you, I am the last woman you would ever have to worry about when it comes to anything remotely sexual regarding Denzel. Come on, you know it's not like that between me and him." Charm realized how crazy she was being.

"You're right. I'm so sorry. And it's so dumb. The man isn't even mine. I just-"

"You don't have to explain," Brianna said. "We'll talk later. Get dressed." Even though she was a little iffy about what was going on with Charm and Denzel, Brianna knew they were both feeling each other hard. But something about the way Charm reacted to Brianna seeing Denzel naked was another affirmation that Charm wasn't looking to make Denzel her rebound. It could get much more serious if they kept at it.

"Where are we going?" Charm asked as she moisturized her skin before slipping on her underwear and her bra.

"Denzel is treating us both to massages," She smiled. Charm looked at her.

"Seriously?" Brianna handed her the card and flower Denzel had left her. Charm took the rose and smelled it before opening the card and reading it.

Sometimes even a beautiful woman needs time to feel beautiful. Follow Brianna everywhere. And don't let her drive you crazy.

Charm laughed at the words he wrote. She was so impressed that he was doing something like this for her.

"He's so sweet," She mumbled.

"Even though you're spending time with me instead of him, he wants you to be pampered. Especially all the shit that's been going on with you."

"That's what so sweet of him. I would be satisfied with him getting in my guts but I can see why he would give me an alternative." Brianna rolled her eyes.

"I bet he can get in your guts with that monster I saw in that drawing."

"Hey!" Charm snapped. "Don't bring that up again! Because that means you're thinking about it! And well I don't want you thinking about it. Because it's mine to think about!"

"Charm calm down!" Brianna laughed. "Get dressed. Our appointment is in half an hour." Charm chuckled and quickly went about doing her hair. She left it out today instead of putting it in her short ponytail. She put on a pair of nice jeans with sandals and a crop top.

"Great you look sexy. That's the type of shit you should be wearing around Terrell. Make his ass regret what the fuck he did to you."

"You know what. I think I will do something like that. Every time I have to go see his ass," Charm scoffed.

"I still wanna fuck his ass up, but you playing," Brianna said. The both of them headed towards the front door after Charm grabbed her purse and was ready to go.

"And Denzel is such a quiet man, and look what he has as a best friend," Charm chuckled. "A freaking psycho." Brianna busted out laughing.

"If not for me, he would be bored all the time. Ain't like his girlfriend was going to take time out just to paint with him or do anything he likes." Charm shook her head. She figured Gabrielle probably wouldn't want to do anything of the sort. Not like Terrell would paint with her either.

"When was the last time you did something relaxing besides paint?" Brianna asked her on their way to the spa in her car.

"Well, three months back I tried to have a picnic with Terrell in our backyard. That was basically ruined because of how I noticed my husband looking at the woman who was supposed to be a guest in our house. He was so blatantly into her it's amazing how I was so stupid to think they wouldn't eventually be hooking up. In the end I'm the one that looks like the real clown. And she's giving him something that I can't."

"That's bullshit Charm and you know it. Looking and actually touching is very two different things. For instance that's twice I've seen Denzel's dick but that doesn't make me want to touch it. Terrell made a conscience decision to fuck her and so he did. Regardless if he looked or not. And do you really want to be pregnant by a lying, cheating, scumbag?" Brianna asked her.

"Like seriously, would you take him back despite the way he talks to you and how he treats you, all because you were pregnant?"

"Well, it would be hard not to! I mean, being pregnant for me means so much more than you know Brianna. It's hard to say if I would get back with him for sure, but I know I'd keep it. And raising a kid without its father, I don't want to become another statistic." Brianna felt that she couldn't relate because she'd never been in that situation to even think about becoming a mom. And she was sure the decision was hard for Charm, but she just knew Charm was worth more than how Terrell treated her.

"All I know Charm is that you're worth more than how he treats you. No matter if you're carrying his baby or not. In fact, if you were pregnant it would make it a whole lot worse if he was disrespecting you the way he does. If a woman is carrying a baby for a man, he should be worshipping the ground she's walking on." Charm crossed her arms and sighed. She rubbed her eyes as she thought.

"What? What'd I say wrong?"

"Nothing," Charm said. "You said everything right."

"So what's the problem?" Brianna asked.

"Because that's how he's treating Destiny. Worshipping her

because she's carrying his kid. But at the same time he wants me back. I can't tell him to cut ties with her if our marriage is ever going to work again because the woman is carrying his kid. And really that's what hurts the most."

"So you want to be with him?" Brianna asked softly. Charm got quiet. She didn't speak again until they pulled up in the parking lot of the spa. Brianna shut the car off and waited for Charm to speak. It was clear she was trying to sort her words out in her head.

"I wouldn't be with him again," Charm said finally.

"I feel like you have much more to add onto that," Brianna said.

"If I tell you this, promise not to tell Denzel. This is just between us. As females."

"Of course," Brianna smiled. Charm turned in the seat to face Brianna.

"I didn't just have one miscarriage," Charm said. "I've had four." Brianna gasped and covered her mouth. "So that woman he got pregnant was supposed to be our surrogate. Only she was supposed to be carrying my egg and his sperm."

"Oh my god," She breathed. Charm brushed the tear that left her eye.

"And I was just thinking to myself. What if, instead of four miscarriages, I have four beautiful babies and my husband cheated on me, in my own home with a woman I thought I trusted. Would I be so quick to up and leave him? So it's not so much on if I want to be with him, it's a question on if I should give up on 5 years of our marriage that easy to a man I've known for ten years. The same man that for ten years I've only been with sexually until Denzel. And it's so weird because Terrell wasn't my first and I experienced another man before him, but when it came to us dating I was very diligent in not cheating. But did I give up on him too quickly?"

"Honey, time does not matter! Surely with children in the picture I can see where you'd be apprehensive, but as an amazing, beautiful woman you don't have to force yourself to be with a man you don't want to be with because of time. He's the one that flushed your five year marriage down the drain. Not you." Charm took a deep breath and wiped her eyes.

"Thanks for listening," She smiled.

"I'm here for you! I'm Denzel's best friend but I can be your friend too. I've got enough love to go around. And you need friendship right now." Charm nodded. That was the truth.

"Let's forget about Terrell trifling ass and enjoy the spa day your new boo is paying for," Brianna smiled.

"I hear that!" Charm laughed. They got out of Brianna's car and walked happily towards the spa.

For the whole afternoon, they got massages, and manicures and pedicures. All in all, they were treated like royalty. Charm couldn't recall the last time she did something like this with another female no less. And she was so appreciative of Denzel for making this happen. Spending time with Brianna took her mind off of a lot of things. In their white robes, they sipped champagne and got pedicures while eating strawberries.

"After this we're going to the mall," Brianna said. "And we've got hair appointments. When was the last time you did your hair?" Brianna asked her. Charm rolled her eyes.

"Not for a while! I usually get it trimmed to retain my neck length but now that it's a little bit longer I'm starting to like it. Don't tell me Denzel is paying for us to get our hair done?"

"Yes he is!" Brianna said. "You don't have to get a trim but you probably need a wash and some moisture up in there."

"Stop tryna play me," Charm demanded while she laughing. "My head not dry!"

"Shit, could have fooled me!" Charm reached over and slapped her playfully.

"I swear I can't stand you!" Charm nearly fell out of the pedicure chair dying with laughter.

"Whatever girl," Brianna smiled. "We're gonna get our hair done and then Denzel said he wants to buy you something cute."

"Why though?"

"Because he wants to," Brianna said. "And shit, if he wants to, just let him."

"With the way Gabrielle acted, she made it seem as if he never got her anything. But now he's doing all this for me."

"No he got Gabrielle a lot of shit. And he wanted to go on some bomb ass dates with her. But she was just too much. She always wanted more you know? Like if he took her shopping she would head straight for the designer sections and try to spend 400 dollars on a Gucci handbag knowing well he didn't make money like that. And then when he told her no, she'd throw a fit and act like he never wanted to get her anything." Charm shook her head.

"I promise you Charm, if you can appreciate the little things he does for you, then there's nothing he won't do for you. And that's what he values most."

"Is it wrong of me to be a little mad when she comes around him? I feel like it's not my place, but the other day she was talking junk in my face at the gallery and I just wanted to strangle her ass!"

"What the hell was she saying?"

"That I'm only here temporarily and once Denzel wants something real he's going back to her. Then of course I got insecure because what if he does go back to her? I mean they've been together as long as me and Terrell. And they've taken each other's virginities and shit."

"Oh please. She's full of shit," Brianna scoffed. "And you see the way you were coming at me this morning for looking at a drawing that you created?! And it wasn't even the real thing? I don't know why you ain't pop Gabrielle in the mouth."

"Because like I said, it didn't seem like my place. Denzel isn't…mine."

"But you'd be heated if he was hooking up with Gabrielle right now and using me to keep you distracted so you didn't find out right?" Charm sat straight up and glared at Brianna.

"Are you serious?" Charm whispered. "Is that what he's doing?!" Brianna watched as tears formed in Charm's eyes.

"No, no! I was only saying it to make a point. That's not what he's doing I promise." Brianna quickly realized her plan had failed. Charm wiped her eyes to hide the fact that she nearly just cried over a man that wasn't even hers. What was her problem?

"Don't ever do that again," Charm mumbled.

"I just wanted to prove you're already territorial as fuck. But the tears I didn't expect. What was that all about?"

"The thought of a man deceiving me again," Charm shrugged. "Plus, Denzel is different from Terrell. His betrayal would hurt more now than anything."

"What makes him different?" Brianna asked.

"From the moment I first laid eyes on him I was captivated. I pushed that all the back of my head though because I was a married woman. But spending time with him and seeing how he cared, and how he liked to listen, and the times where Terrell drove me crazy and he was there to be the friend to lean on. So when Terrell betrayed me and Denzel was there letting my cry in his arms, something just clicked inside my brain. And I don't know, I couldn't just put on that platonic front anymore. I knew I wanted his flesh and that I wanted to feel something more than his friendship. We have so much more to give each other I know, but it's real hopeful to think that I have someone who I can feel myself falling deeply for."

"There's something you have that Gabrielle didn't have. I don't know what it is, only Denzel knows. But I know that even when he and Gabrielle were mad at each other and giving each other space, he has never entertained another woman. But when he saw you and he was speechless, that was his defining moment." Charm sat back and began to daydream about Denzel. Even though she was having fun with Brianna, she couldn't help but think about him. She hadn't even gotten to see him before he up and left earlier.

"What?" Brianna asked seeing how Charm got quiet.

"Has he texted you?"

"Yeah, he's checking in to make sure we're good."

"Why doesn't he text me?" Charm pouted. Brianna gave her a look. She knew why Denzel wasn't texting Charm but she was given strict orders not to tell her anything.

"He says he doesn't want to bother you. He hasn't really texted me that much either."

"That's bull," Charm crossed her arms. "And I didn't even get to see his face before he left the loft earlier."

"I'm pretty sure he'll look the same," Brianna teased. Charm rolled her eyes.

"Maybe I should call him? Just to hear his voice." She reached for the pocket of the robe so she could get her phone.

"No!" Brianna said reaching over to grab her cell phone.

"Give that back!" Charm demanded.

"We're having a girl's day," Brianna said. "And if I let you call him, the two of you might be on the phone forever. Nobody got time for that. You'll see him later relax. Not like he's going to disappear." Charm crossed her arms like a child that didn't get what they wanted.

"Wait a minute, are you actually missing him?" Brianna asked. Charm slowly uncrossed her arms. She didn't attribute her attitude to the fact that she missed him.

"Well...ever since I left Terrell I've seen Denzel almost every single day. So maybe I do miss him," She admitted.

"You probably only miss the way his dick feels inside you."

Charm sucked her teeth.

"As a matter of fact, that's not what I miss!" She snapped. "What time is it, 2? Right now if we weren't at the gallery or on the way to the gallery, he'd probably be letting me lay on him while I sketch. Which I am learning I love resting on his chest with my sketchbook." Charm realized how she sounded. Damn. She had it bad.

"You know what. Let's get this day finished up so you can go cuddle with your boo. Can't take you nowhere," Brianna shook her head. Charm rolled her eyes again.

"Let's get the facial then we can go get our hair done," Charm said.

"Sounds like a plan." The two women finished up their pedicures before going to get a European facial. But before they left the spa, one of the services they provided made Charm stop in her tracks.

"I don't know about you, but I wanna do that," Charm said pointing towards the room. They'd finished their facials and was ready to get dressed to leave, but Charm didn't want to leave before doing this one last thing.

"V-Steaming? Please tell me that's not what I think it is."

"It's a yoni steam room!" Charm said excitedly. "I've always wanted to do one. And they say it had some positive effects on your uterus and it gives your yoni a new life. I think Denzel would appreciate it."

"I bet he would," Brianna mumbled as Charm dragged her towards the room where they removed their underwear and sat on huge comfy chairs that had holes in them. After five minutes of sitting in the chair, a fragrance filled the room before Brianna felt the warm steam. Brianna jumped at the feeling and looked at Charm.

"Whoa," She smiled "This feels good!" The both of them laughed and continued talking as they got their yoni's steamed. That was the last thing they did at the spa and when it was over, Charm couldn't help but think she couldn't wait to let Denzel feel the effects of the steam later that night.

Once they left the spa, the both of them got back in Brianna's car to head to the mall. Once again, Charm hadn't went shopping in a while. She wasn't going to bullshit. Terrell was the obvious breadwinner. He paid most of the bills and he never complained about it. Whatever money Charm made, she contributed what she could to the bills and that was it. Between her art supplies and the things she needed to host her classes, she didn't have the extra money to go shopping and she wasn't going to ask her husband because he was already footing all the bills.

Now being in a mall and able to just buy something nice, even if it was only three items made her feel good. On top of that, she and Brianna laughed up and down the mall like hooligans. By the time they were done, Charm had purchased a nice sundress and a new pair of wedges.

"Look you should get this too," Brianna told her, showing her the calf length peach colored off the shoulder dress.

"Wow this is pretty," Charm said dreamily, looking at the little accents of the dress that made it sparkle.

"Get it! It's within the budget. And then we can get our hair done."

"But where would I even wear this to?"

"I'm sure if you buy it then you'll find a reason to wear it. In fact, why don't we go out tonight? You can wear it then."

"On a Thursday?"

"Get the damn dress and let's go," Brianna snapped getting annoyed with her questions. "As a matter of fact. What size are you? Two?" Brianna began looking through the rack to find Charm's size. Charm busted out in laughter.

"How about a 6," Charm stated. "Never have I been a size 2."

"How unfortunate," Brianna scoffed. "Let's go. We don't want to get to the salon too late now."

Brianna went to the front and paid for their items with Denzel's credit card. He'd given her a firm limit to spend on each activity they did for the day, and thankfully they were still on budget. The last thing Brianna wanted to do was spend that man's money knowing he didn't acquire it easily. Not only was Denzel showing Charm he could pamper her, the time Brianna was spending with Charm really helped Brianna scope the woman out. At work, Charm was sweet, kind, funny, and very talented. She wore her heart on her sleeve and Brianna didn't think Charm would ever purposely bring harm to Denzel. But when a women's heart got broken, a lot of shit changed. And Brianna just wanted to know what really went on in Charm's head. But from the looks of it, her best friend was going to have an incredible woman when they were both ready for commitment. All in all, Charm wasn't like his ex-girlfriend, and that said more about Charm than anything.

While they sat under the dryers at the salon, they spoke about nothing too serious and giggled and laughed. Brianna loved Denzel to death, he was her brother. But to have a female friend was something so new to her and it was refreshing. Any female friend she had in the past was only her friend because they were trying to get close to Denzel enough to see if he would cheat on his girlfriend for a quickie with them. Little did they know, Denzel was one faithful son of a gun who'd never step out on Gabrielle. Denzel was king of keeping his dick where it belonged. But even though Charm and Denzel was hooking up, Charm hadn't used Brianna to get close to Denzel. She did that of her own accord.

It was almost 7 by the time they pulled up to Brianna's home. Charm had never been there so she was eager to see what it looked like. Just like Denzel, Brianna lived in a loft only 15 minutes away from Denzel's place. With silky hair from their blowouts, fresh faces, freshly steamed yoni's, and hands full of bags for the day's adventure, they climbed into the elevator and took it up to the loft. Unlike Denzel's place, Brianna's loft was filled with color. In the living room the light blue curtains matched the blue fluffy rug on the ground under her expensive looking glass table. Her kitchen was decorated red, with red curtains, and red floor mats. Charm was impressed by the design but had to admit it was so like Brianna.

"This place is so cute," She complimented.

"It was hard getting it just the way I wanted it."

"I love it. You did a good job decorating." Charm saw when Brianna looked at her watch.

"The place I think we should go to opens in 30 minutes. If we go just as it opens we can get a good spot. So let's move it."

"Damn why didn't you say something before?" Charm asked. She followed Brianna to the bedroom where she dumped their clothes on the bed. Luckily Charm had bought new underwear and didn't have to worry that she had none at Brianna's house. She went in for a quick shower before Brianna. When she came back Brianna was ready to do her makeup.

"Please don't make me look like a clown," Charm retorted. "And I hardly ever wear makeup anyway. Is this necessary?"

"Well, Denzel doesn't like a lot of makeup in the first place, but I'm just giving you a little concealer and some blush with a nice lip. It'll be fine."

"What's Denzel got to do with us having a ladies night out?" Charm asked.

"He might be missing your ass just like you missing his, and just pop up. Either way you should look hot."

"If being hot didn't keep my husband interested then-"

"If you bring up that lowlife man again Charm I swear I'll strangle you."

"Sorry. I can't help it sometimes."

"Yeah well you need to. It's not like Denzel is bringing up Gabrielle every two seconds." Charm shook her head.

"You know he told me that our sex wasn't meaningful? That we're just fuck buddies? Which I guess he's sort of right about that, but I don't just give my body to anyone."

"I'm sure he didn't mean it in a disrespectful way. And then he is kind of right like you said." Charm huffed out in anger.

"Don't do that. You're gonna mess me up," Brianna exclaimed. Charm stilled her facial expressions and let Brianna do her work. After two minutes of silence, Brianna spoke.

"Do the doctors know why you kept miscarrying?" She asked.

"No. It always happened by the time I was four months. That early they don't know the reason for it. They've ran tests and nothing has come up dangerously wrong with my uterus and there's nothing wrong with my eggs. But I suppose by body just can't handle supporting a baby."

"I can't even imagine how difficult that is for you," Brianna sighed. "And as hard as it is for me to say, if you and Denzel want to use me as a surrogate then fine." Charm pulled back and opened her eyes. She spotted the smirk on Brianna's face before the woman started laughing openly.

"Jerk!" Charm laughed punching her.

"I can't believe I just said that. Just thinking about Denzel's sperm in me gives me the fucking heebie jeebies," She shivered.

"First off, we're nowhere near baby talk and secondly he doesn't even know I can't have kids. He just knows I had one miscarriage. And after what Gabrielle did to him, I don't think he's thinking about-" Charm clamped her hand over her mouth before she finished her sentence.

"What? Finish that!" Brianna ordered.

"I'm sorry I can't. And I've already said too much. It's really not my place to tell you." Brianna grunted in anger. She returned to doing Charm's makeup and the silence resumed. If ever Denzel knew that Charm told Brianna his business like that she didn't think he would appreciate it.

After her makeup, Brianna took Charm's hair down from its pin curls, then helped Charm into her fitted dress. In all that happened to her, in the moment Charm didn't feel anything but beautiful. And she didn't care that her husband was a cheat. She actually felt like a woman.

"Wait a minute, when are you going to get dressed?" Charm asked Brianna realizing the woman had only doted on her and not taken time out to even get dressed.

"Oh, I'm not," Brianna smiled.

"What?" Charm was confused. Brianna looked at her phone.

"Come. It's time to go."

"Time to go where?! I thought it was me and you tonight?!" Brianna grabbed Charm's hand and led her towards the front door. Charm couldn't do anything but follow behind her trying not to trip in her wedge heels. They left the loft and took the elevator down to street level.

"Remember, stop bringing up Terrell. No one hates a sore loser."

"I am not a sore loser," Charm snapped.

"Right. So then stop talking about the game you lost and focus on the one you're playing at the moment." Charm sucked her teeth at the metaphor.

"I still don't know what-" Brianna dragged Charm outside and pushed her in front. Charm gasped when she saw Denzel leaning on the hood of his car waiting for her.

Chapter Thirteen

Charm was speechless as she gazed at Denzel. Like Brianna said in the morning, he indeed went to get a shapeup and the way his newly sharp lines framed his dreads was sexy enough to make Charm drool. He wore a black V-neck, with a deep burgundy blazer and black fitted jeans that weren't too tight but not too loose. They were just right. His hair was pulled back from his face like it always was.

"Thanks for keeping her company today," Denzel spoke to Brianna.

"Of course D. You know I got your back. Now go on and have fun. I'm gonna watch some Netflix." Brianna waved at then and retreated back inside the building. Charm couldn't help but to keep gazing at Denzel. Damn he looked so fucking good.

"Wow Charm, you look amazing," Denzel said leaning off the hood. He walked up to her and took her hand.

"What is the meaning of this?" she asked.

"Can't a man take you on a date?" he questioned. Charm realized he'd set the day up for this exact moment. Denzel led her towards his car. But he could hardly take his eyes off her. She was so radiant in that dress that matched her skin complexion with ease. Her makeup was light and her hair was curled at the ends still neck length long. Denzel wanted to run his hands through her silkiness but he didn't want to ruin the curls. He led her inside his car before going to the other side and getting in. Charm sat back comfortably loving the feel of being near him. He was playing throwback jams, setting the mood.

"You're so beautiful," Denzel said turning to look at her. Charm felt herself blushing.

"Thank you," She smiled. "You're looking very daddyish yourself." Denzel laughed at her.

"Stop it," He chuckled. He turned forward to start driving but Charm stopped him.

"Denzel," she called. He looked over at her and the moment he did, Charm leaned over and kissed him smack dab on the lips. But Charm should have known there was nothing like a simple kiss on the lips. Charm couldn't stop pecking on his lips before he finally held her behind the neck and pushed his tongue in her mouth. Charm sucked his tongue and allowed him to suck hers as they traded breaths in their sloppy kiss. His mouth was sweet like it always was and she could taste the minty flavor of his Carmex that he rubbed on his succulent lips. Someone in a car next to them beeped their horn making them jerk apart.

"Damn Charm," Denzel said, wiping her lipstick from his lips and fixing his arousal in his pants. Charm pulled out a small mirror from her purse and made sure her nude lipstick wasn't smeared all over her face.

"That was only supposed to be a peck," She said innocently as he pulled away from the curb and headed towards their destination.

"Yeah well you should have stopped yourself," Denzel accused.

"Not my fault your lips taste so damn good. And hey! You could have stopped too. You started the tongue action." Denzel smirked. He couldn't argue with that one. But once again, how was a man not to give some tongue when the woman clearly wanted it?

"I plead the fifth," Denzel finally said. Charm laughed at him. Man, he loved to hear her laughter. He'd never been given pleasure by just hearing someone laugh. Not even Gabrielle. This was too different for him. But he did like it. And that's why he always wanted her laughing.

On the drive to their destination, they talked casually about the day the both of them had. Denzel was happy to hear that she loved the time at the spa and even just simply shopping. Those were things she didn't do often at all and it was nice to get out and feel like a woman. Denzel wanted her to feel that way because of the weight she had on her shoulders from the way her own husband talked to her. Nothing was more important than for her to feel like she was a woman.

Charm gasped when they pulled up to a large building packed with people lined up to go in. The place had those lights that shone all around it, illuminating the spot like it was the only one on the block. Charm knew of the place but she'd never, ever been. She just didn't have the time.

"Wait? Are we going here? Do you know I've always wanted to come here?"

"Yes we're going here. And I know you've always wanted to

come here because I asked Jason," Denzel smiled. "Plus its real cool you wanted to come to this place because I've always wanted to come. And well when I told Gabrielle I'd bring her, she wasn't enthused. I guess this is a place for artists and old souls to enjoy."

"I'm so excited!" Charm bounced in her seat. Denzel appreciated the actual excitement rolling off her. It made him pumped to be experiencing the place with her.

Madame Jojo's was one of the most popular jazz spots in town. Not only did they have a live band that created incredible music but their food was amazing, and comfort of the place made it prime location for date nights. And Denzel had to admit, as he walked the red carpet towards the entrance of the club, he felt so prideful to have Charm at his side. As they walked, men turned and looked at Charm and the fact that she was on his arm just gave him that extra pep in his step.

Denzel gave his name to the man at the front kiosk. He smiled at them and then motioned inside where a waitress was waiting to escort them to their booth. Charm was looking all around the dark place, lighted by dark blue light amplifying the fact that it was a blues lounge. The saxophone player was playing his heart out on the stage. Charm felt her hips begin to move at the sensual sounds coming from his instrument.

"This place is so nice," Charm gasped. Denzel held the small of her waist and kissed her cheek. When they got to the booth Denzel waited until she was sitting before he sat across from her. The waitress poured them champagne and left them with strawberries until they were ready to order dinner.

"This is great," Charm smiled lifting her glass. Denzel did the same and they toasted to a great night. Another waitress came by to take their orders.

"Should I get the shrimp?" Denzel asked her. "It sounds good."

"Yes it does. But if you get the shrimp and grits you won't be able to kiss me."

"Damn you gonna do me like that girl?" Denzel smirked.

"No, didn't mean it like that," Charm laughed. "I'm allergic to shellfish. Highly allergic. So even if you eat it and then kiss me, I can still have a reaction."

"Aw, I'm sorry baby girl." Denzel looked at the waitress. "I'll have the steak. Because I'm definitely kissing on her tonight. I mean, look at her." The waitress laughed at him and took his order.

"And for you miss?" She asked Charm.

"I think I'll do the steak as well," Charm smiled. "I love my meat." She gave Denzel a look when she said that. The waitress figured it was an insider and didn't even bother to ask. She finished with pouring them more champagne before she walked off.

"Stop being naughty," Denzel smiled. Charm picked up one of the strawberries then leaned forward to feed it to him. He took the fruit and ate it from her fingers. Eating the strawberry reminded Denzel of going down on Charm. Licking her sweet insides slowly and letting her taste roll over his tongue. It was hard for him to sit there and act like he didn't want to devour her dessert right in the middle of their table. But the point of the date was to not to continue to explore her sexually. He had to explore her mentally too.

"What are you thinking?" Charm asked him.

"Let me not say," He smiled. "It wasn't that innocent of a thought. And I'm trying to control myself." Charm smiled at him. Even without words he was making her feel so beautiful by the way he looked at her. She didn't realize how important that was until now. Denzel picked up a strawberry and fed her this time. She likewise sucked on his finger.

"Tell me about your childhood," Denzel said to her. Charm chuckled.

"I was a goofy little kid," She laughed. "I knew I wanted to be an artist. I drew on everything in my damn house and no matter how many times my mother whooped my butt I kept doing it. So in the garage her and my dad made me my own art studio. They bought me all these art supplies and canvases and I was free to draw and paint on everything. The only catch was that I had to start earning my own money to keep buying all the things I needed. So I would make lemonade and go around town selling it. I would do odd jobs for the old ladies in the neighborhoods and my parents gave me money every time I brought home a good grade. So they taught me that if I wanted to be an artist I wasn't to expect a daily paycheck, and I wasn't to expect immediate success. And I'm thankful they taught me that."

"Wow, that's amazing. But I never hear you talk about your parents now. Especially what's going on with Terrell? You haven't reached out to them." For the first time, Denzel saw the smile waver on Charm's face. He could tell what she was about to say wasn't going to be good.

"When I was 20, I went home to visit my mom and I knew she'd be home. I just didn't expect her to be humping a strange man in her and my dad's bed."

"Holy shit," Denzel gasped.

"I was pissed at her. I couldn't stop yelling, I threw things, I was so fucking angry. I looked up to my mother. I thought she was the most amazing woman ever. And everyone wants to talk about how the black man always cheats. But no one ever sheds light on the black woman who do their black men dirty! And to make it worse that man my mother was sleeping around with had a wife himself. And that wife found out just what my mother was doing. She came to our house and broadcasted it to the world. My father found out and it tore him apart. My mother couldn't handle the drama so she packed up all her things and rode off into the night. I didn't speak to her again until Terrell proposed. I was the bigger woman and invited her to my wedding but she never came. I haven't seen her since the day I caught her being unfaithful."

"What about your dad?"

"He was depressed for a long time. But then he met a woman in the Bahamas when he went to take a vacation. She's beautiful, chocolate and they fell in love. So after my wedding he moved down to the Bahamas to live with his newfound woman. I couldn't be happier for him. And calling him to tell him that my husband cheated on me, or that he won't be a grandfather is too much for me to handle. So I haven't told him. I just want him to keep being happy."

"He does deserve to know if things get too complicated," Denzel said. "And maybe even if you're a grown woman you need your father."

"I need my father to be happy and that's it. I mean, have you called your mom and told her that Gabrielle aborted her grandbaby?"

"No, I didn't. But for the same reason I didn't tell Brianna. My mom will come back here guns a blazing and not caring what law she broke."

"I wonder what your mom is like. To have to deal with your dad. With him being an alcoholic."

"It was tough on her. Tough on us all. My dad was a strange man. He'd get pissed, drink his life away and come home to beat the crap out of me. I always asked him, why are you hitting me? I haven't done anything. And he would glare at me, and I'd never forget these words."

"What'd he say?" Charm asked leaning into him. Denzel rolled his neck.

"He said, 'because I wanna beat the shit out of someone. And the only person here is you or your mother. And you're never to put your hands on a female. So I'm gonna beat the shit out of you till I pass the fuck out.'" Charm covered her mouth.

"That's horrible," She said.

"It's strange because he's teaching me how to be a man while still beating the hell out of me just because he needed a conduit for his own downfall. But my mom wasn't weak. She fought him every time he laid his hands on me. And if not for me drawing that's all I would have in my life. Fighting. And it just burns the shit out of me that I've become just like him."

"No you haven't! You're nowhere near being an alcoholic."

"I meant his anger. I've inherited it."

"Even so, you don't use your anger as an excuse to drink or to beat on someone. You find a way to channel it and that's more than he ever did." Charm reached over and held his hands. There they sat in silence, holding hands and gazing into each other's eyes. It felt like they had some sort of telepathic thing going on because even if they weren't speaking it was like they were still trading stories with each other. Charm could see Denzel as a child, beaten and bruised but still retreating to his room and draw anything that came to his mind. And Denzel could see Charm having to deal with knowing her mother was the one who was the cheater and now having to face the fact that she was dealing with the same thing. But she wasn't retreating like her mother did. She was facing it head on.

A throat cleared. Charm and Denzel snapped from their own world and looked up to see the waitress holding both their dinners. Reluctantly, they let go of their hands to allow their food to be set in front of them. The steak was dripping in gravy and they couldn't wait to dig in.

"I hadn't really eaten all day," Charm said taking a bite of the steak. She moaned at the pleasurable taste.

"It's real good." Denzel wanted to eat but for a moment he just sat there staring at Charm. He leaned his elbow on the table and rested his chin in his palm. He just gazed at her like a child gazing at something wondrous that he couldn't explain. Charm felt his eyes and looked up from her food.

"What?" she asked. She began touching her face to see if she had sauce on her face.

"No, you're fine," Denzel said dreamily. "You're amazing." Charm tilted her head and looked at him curiously.

"So you're being a creep because…"

"I'm mesmerized. I'm sorry if I'm making you uncomfortable."

"It's not that I'm uncomfortable. I'm just not used to it. Like I said before, Terrell doesn't look at me the way you look at me."

"Shame on him," Denzel shook his head. "I just can't get enough of your beauty. It's almost like I'm the nerd and you're the popular girl and I can't believe you're actually on a date with me."

"Oh please!" Charm fanned him off. "By the looks of your ex, I should be the one in shock." Denzel rolled his eyes and laughed at her. He cut into his steak.

"And you evaded it before but I still wanna know if I'm better in the sack than she is. I've got to know if I have to step my game up." Denzel began eating and didn't say anything. Charm gave him a look.

"I'm serious Denzel! Tell me!" Denzel smiled and wiped his mouth.

"She's pretty good in bed. Not much she won't do."

"And what about me?" Charm asked.

"Your moans are real. Her moans…let's just say I know the difference between when she's having a real orgasm and when she's not. I'm a man, but I don't need my ego stroked. I appreciate genuine moans. And your pussy feels, really, really good." Charm smiled, loving that he enjoyed her as much as he would enjoy Gabrielle. But she still wanted to be better.

"It's not a competition though," he reminded her.

"Sure, if you think that," Charm teased.

They continued to eat their dinner, still talking in between bites, sharing stories from each phase of their life. The both of them felt so honored to be learning more about each other. And the fact that they could sit across from each other, so enthralled with their stories meant that their relationship wasn't just about the sex. Knowing Denzel wanted to pick her brain about any and everything made Charm feel confident. It made her feel wanted, and important. As the night went on, the music never stopped playing. And when the saxophonist paired with the jazz singer, a beautiful melody trickled from their instruments. Denzel saw when Charm began to tilt side to side as he fed her their dessert. He looked towards the dancefloor filled with couples slowly rocking to the tender music. Feeling it was his duty, Denzel stood from the table. He fixed himself and held his hand out for Charm to take it.

"Dance with me," He said softly. She took his hand without hesitation. He led her to the dancefloor and secured them in a spot directly in front of the stage. At first Charm just stood in front of him not sure how he wanted to dance. Their first dance ever had been spur of the moment, fun, and silly. But that was when they were simply friends. Denzel wrapped an arm around her waist and pulled her close.

"This won't be like the first time," He murmured. She smiled and wrapped her arms around his neck. They were so close it would look like their bodies were meant to blend together. All her curves fit with his curves, and his embrace was warm and cozy.

"I feel like we're at the 6th grade dance," Charm mumbled. Denzel chuckled and took one of her arms from around his neck. They assumed the dancing position, still very close together. One of her arms around his neck. One of his arms around her waist. And they used their free hand to hold each other's hand.

"Feel better?" He asked.

"Now I feel like a woman." Denzel pressed her deeper into his body and buried his nose into her neck.

"You have the sweetest smell on this planet," He whispered. Charm could hear herself whimpering with pleasure as she felt his arousal embedded into her stomach. The way he moved her on the dancefloor made her feel like a princess.

"Denzel," She whispered. He removed his nose from her neck so he could look her in the eye.

"Yes baby girl?"

"I know it's too soon. And I know it might never happen. But-but just for the comfort I wanna know…"

"Know what?"

"What would you say to me in this moment if you wanted me to be your wife? If in another universe it was you who asked me out first instead of Terrell. If it was you who got down on one knee and asked me to be yours forever." Denzel let out a smooth breath. His hold on her never wavered nor did his stare.

"I would tell you that when I look at you, you give me butterflies. That when the sun rises I want to be in your arms. And when the sun sets, I want to be in your arms. And when I'm away from you I can't stop thinking about you. Wondering if you're happy or you're sad. And that no matter how it may rain on you, I want to be the sunshine in your life. Because even when you're down you bring me so much light. I would say to you that I want to be with a woman who knows no fear of the truth. A woman who would rather have me incredibly angry at her rather than to lie to me about something she knows would hurt me. I would say that I want a woman ready to walk through fire with me and not afraid to be burned. And I would tell you that I want a woman who's not afraid to be with a man that's not perfect. And even when times are rough, she can always leave-" Denzel let her go to spin her around before bringing her back tight to his body.

"But she'll know when that sun is setting to come right back into my arms." Denzel dipped her over in time with the soft music before picking her back up. He raised her chin.

"Then I would kiss you oh so tenderly and ask you to give me a chance to have you forever." Charm felt a tear leak from her eye. Denzel kissed it away, noting that even her tears tasted sweet.

Charm took a deep breath trying to keep her nose from running. She rested her head against his chest to hide the fact that she was crying yet again because she was reminded of something from Terrell. Her real proposal wasn't like what Denzel had just given her. At no point in time had Terrell declared that much things about her that he liked. But Charm was in love with him and was blind to anything else. All she could see was that a man thought she was good enough to be his wife. And Charm thought that was okay. Obviously now it wasn't.

"Why do you cry?" He asked leaning to whisper in her ear. Charm couldn't even answer him. She didn't know what words she would use to explain why the hell she was crying over Terrell when she had Denzel in her arms.

"It's stupid," She mumbled.

"Nothing you have to say is stupid baby," He told her. "I know it's because of Terrell. And that's okay. Tell me."

"His proposal just wasn't like that. And even in our years of marriage, he hasn't confessed anything like that to me. And well, even if he didn't say it, it's not like his actions were showing it. But

I'm tired of having to tell you over and over and my husband wasn't what I thought he would be." The crazy part was Charm wasn't so sure that she would have even left Terrell if he never cheated. She would have just dealt with anything that was happening with them. They were after all just trying to start a family and shit just all fell apart.

"I guess it took you showing me certain things to realize Terrell never gave me those things," Charm said. Denzel pulled her face from his chest and made her look at him. He said no words. He simply leaned down to kiss her. But this wasn't just no peck. His intention was to slide his tongue into her mouth from jump. And when he did he pushed deep to take that subtle control of her mouth. Charm nearly crumbled to the ground and if he wasn't holding her she would be down and out looking stupid on the floor. But the way his lips took hold of hers and the way he massaged her mouth with his tongue was enough to make any girl weak. And Charm was a sucker and just succumbed. She could feel her clit throbbing through her thin panties, beating to the same sounds of the music vibrating around them.

"Den-" He let go of her lips for a millisecond and she tried to tell him to stop because she couldn't control herself. But he only let her up to change positions. He cupped her neck with both his hands and deepened the kiss. Oh fuck the dancing. They weren't moving in time to the beat anymore. At least not their bodies. But their tongues danced like hell to the music. Even when the music stopped their tongues didn't. They could hear everyone applauding the musicians but they literally couldn't stop.

"Denzel stop," Charm begged.

"I know, shit," He groaned, pecking her lips. "I can't. When she pressed her body to his she felt his arousal. Charm slowly eased out of his touch and pulled her face from his hold. He took a deep breath and tried to control himself and not push back into her. There they stood breathing hard looking at each other.

"I'm gonna need you to walk in front of me," He said lowly. Charm knew why. She nodded and maneuvered in front of him. When they looked up that's when they realized what else their kissing had caught them. Every couple that was on the dancefloor with them was gawking at their display of intimacy. Charm immediately felt herself beginning to blush. She didn't mind PDA, but this was different. Charm cleared her throat and looked up at

Denzel. He was close behind her, his shaft still clearly hardened as he pressed it against her back. Like teenagers, they smiled lowly at everyone and slowly inched off the dancefloor. Charm noticed however that the women were smiling at them, but tossing their mates a look as if expecting more from them. Charm giggled and walked in front of Denzel back to their table. She went to his seat first so he could sit down before going back to hers.

"You alright?" Denzel asked her.

"Hot and bothered, but I'm okay," She smiled.

"Noted," Denzel smiled. They shared another glass of champagne continuing to talk about anything that came to their minds. Charm loved learning more about the man she was so wickedly attracted to. She found that not only did she love how he touched her body, but she was intrigued by those little stories he told her. The both of them were actually very different. They hardly had anything in common, but it was actually making their bond stronger.

"Batman is like the most boring superhero ever," Charm said making a face. Denzel gasped and grabbed his dreads.

"What?! Are you kidding me?! He's like the richest man in Gotham and he doesn't have any random ass powers that he just happen to have. Which means that all the fighting he does is all him. No powers, nothing!"

"Eh, I can still do without." Denzel crossed his arms.

"So what superhero would you prefer? And say superman. I dare you. Give me a reason to spank that ass later." Charm busted out in laughter and slapped the table.

"Storm," Charm said. Denzel nodded and accepted her choice.

"I can take that," He said. "Storm is cool."

"I like her so much I had plans to name one of my kids after her. I think Storm is pretty unisex. I never told Terrell that though, so I doubt he would have liked it."

"Storm is a very....interesting name for a real child," Denzel said. Charm rolled her eyes knowing he would give her that response.

"I mean, with the way these celebrities are naming their kids I don't see a problem with Storm. What? Would you want a Jr. or something?" Denzel smirked at her.

"Well no. And either way I'm the Jr. So if I named my kid Denzel he'd be the third."

"Oh! So you're a junior then! You never said so before!"

"You know who my dad is," Denzel said. "Didn't want you to know we had the same name." Charm reached over and ran her hand against his cheek.

"And because of who my dad is, I'm not gonna stick my kid with his name like I got stuck with it."

"Well how about this question. If you can name your kid after any superhero who would it be? And please don't say Bruce Wayne. Because then I'll be the one to spank you later on." Denzel laughed.

"Come here." He stood and took her hand when she stood. He'd already paid for dinner so there was no need for them to stay at the table. He led her across the dancefloor to the lounge chairs. He sunk down into an empty one and pulled Charm to sit on his lap. They sat comfortably to talk and not have to deal with a table between them.

"There's no superhero whose name is not too weird to name my kid after. My favorite hands down is Black Panther. What am I gonna name my kid? Panther? T'Challa? Black?" Charm began laughing when he said each name. She rested against him and took her time regaining her composure. When he chuckled his chest vibrated through her back. Charm gave a comforting sigh.

"I know you told me you were already confused about your relationship with Gabrielle because she wanted marriage you and didn't yet. But have you ever thought about wanting kids?"

"I knew eventually I'd become a dad, I just hadn't planned it or really thought about it. I feel like I'm still not ready to be a father because I just want to be stable enough to support a kid. I can feel myself getting stable, with the work we do at the company but I just need a little bit more."

"I'll make sure we're getting some good paying gigs. Jason stays on top of it, but now with the three of us I should put in some work to help him."

"We'll all pitch in." Charm involuntarily yawned. Denzel kissed her temple. "Ready to go baby girl?" He asked.

"Kind of, but I just don't want this to end. I've had such a good time. I like being here with you. Enjoying you."

"Just because we leave doesn't mean anything is going to end," He said huskily. He kissed her neck. Charm already knew where this could possibly lead. And then she remembered her Yoni

Steam. Yeah. It was time to go.

"Let's go," She whispered to him. Before she could stand herself, Denzel put his arms under her legs and lift her in his arms as he stood. Again, eyes were on them as Denzel carried her through the place.

"You just love the attention don't you?" Charm teased him. Denzel saw when other women looked at him then gave their men the side eye glance. It was funny but he was only doing this to cater to his woman.

"From you, yeah," He smiled. He kissed her softly and continued out of the lounge. Even though they were leaving their night was far from over. And that's where both Brianna and Jason helped him out again.

Chapter Fourteen

Charm entered Denzel's loft first and noticed immediately the candles lighting the place. She paused and looked back at Denzel. He smiled at her and pushed her inside so he could close the door. Charm just looked around at all the candles and the rose petals on the ground. He seriously went all out for this. Charm was really impressed and she was stunned into silence.

"I-Wow," She breathed. "How'd you even do this?" Charm asked.

"Guess who," He smiled.

"Brianna and Jason," Charm chuckled.

"Follow the roses," Denzel told her. I'll meet you in the bedroom once you call for me."

"Oh really?" Charm nodded and took off, following the trail of the roses. She walked through the house and followed the trail to the bathroom. It was also lighted with candles and flowers. Charm took a note etched into the corner of the mirror and read it. She was instructed to take a quick shower with the special soap that came from the spa she went to earlier and follow the petals once again. She smiled then slowly undressed before washing the light makeup off her face and stepping into the shower. She didn't hear Denzel moving about the house, but she focused on getting clean herself. Once she was done showering, she brushed her teeth, flossed, and then finished with some mouthwash. Wrapped in a towel she followed the petals to where they cast a trail towards his bedroom. The door was open but Denzel wasn't inside.

"Denzel!" She called remembering he told her to call him when she was in the bedroom. His footsteps sounded from further away in the house but when they finally got close and he entered the room, he was dressed in only his boxer briefs. He said nothing to her as he went over to his speaker and turned it on. Charm tried to keep her composure when 'Let's get it on,' filtered from the speaker and Denzel began moving his hips to it. He turned and motioned for Charm to come over to him with his index finger.

Charm dropped the towel to her feet before walking over to him. He took her naked body in his arms and kissed her lightly before caressing her entire body. When she wrapped her arms around his neck, he reached his hands forward and cupped both her ass cheeks. He loved the feel of her in his arms. All her curves were just perfect for him.

"Let's get it on," He mumbled singing the song to her. Charm giggled and grinded against him.

"You know I'm ready," She smiled. He placed his hands behind her thighs and raised her up, carrying her over to the bed. He set her down but he didn't join her.

"Lay down baby girl," He coaxed, pushing her to lay down. Charm laid back, her head towards the head board. Denzel flipped her over so she was laying on her stomach. She felt when his hand slipped off her. When she picked up her head to look at where he was going, he spoke.

"Head down," He ordered. Charm rested her head back down. Instead of looking she listened to what he was doing. She heard him move about the room. Marvin Gaye stopped playing from the speakers and D'Angelo came on. Charm smiled and sighed loving his choice of song. The lyrics to 'Untitled' began and Charm couldn't help but hum along. The bed dipped with Denzel's weight. Something warm dripping onto her back. She naturally jumped but it wasn't out of pain or anything.

The smell of toasted almond brown sugar wafted to her nose. She didn't know what it was, but by the feel of it she figured it was some type of oil. Denzel let the oil drip all long her body. The warm temperature of it made her shiver but not because she was cold. Once her body was properly dripped with oil, Denzel put the bottle down. Starting from her feet, he began massaging the oil into her skin. He tried to rub as gently as possible working up her body. The way she hummed and sighed let him know that she was enjoying the way it felt. He rubbed her ass down but it was only a tease and then he kept moving. He rubbed her back down but he noticed she was trying to thrust her butt against him.

"What you want?" He asked softly in her ear. He moved his hands back down to her ass and massaged her ass cheeks. She moaned and rolled her head to the side. He pressed her cheeks up so he could see her opening. He teased it with his finger. He was trying to wait for the right moment, it was hard not to just center himself at her opening and dive into her tight sheath. He grit hiss teeth to get himself to regain control. He held her at the waist then turned her over. When she looked at him with those hooded eyes, Denzel again fought his control. He picked up the bottle of oil again and began dripping it onto her breasts and then down her stomach. He paid extra special attention to her womanly core. Her hips thrust in the air when she felt the hot oil touch her there. She moaned lowly and tried to touch herself but Denzel didn't allow her to. He bit his lip and began rubbing the oil into her skin starting from her breasts. Her moans became louder as he massaged her breasts. She kept moving her hips even though Denzel wanted her to stay still. But he wasn't going to move faster than he needed to. He slowly moved from her breasts down to her stomach. He purposely evaded the apex of her thighs and continued down her legs. Denzel loved how it drove her crazy. He opened her legs and kneeled in front of them. She was shining like a diamond between her legs, coated with her arousal. Denzel noticed immediately the flowery fragrance that wafted from her opening. She always had a pleasant smell but this was different and just as pleasant. It made his mouth water.

"Take a picture," She teased mocking him from before when he'd told her the same thing when he was sketching his naked body. He grinned at her.

"I'll do one better than that," He teased. He spread her legs wider. He saw her stomach begin to quiver with anticipation. The music switched from D'Angelo to R. Kelly. Perfect timing. 'Seems like you're ready,' blasted through the speakers and it was the perfect sentiment to how they both felt. They're control was just about to snap. And with the way she smelled so sweet, Denzel couldn't wait anymore. He pushed her legs back and leaned over. The first draw of his tongue over her soft clit was euphoric. She was always juicy, but there was something different. The juice that was dripping from her was more than it had ever been. He groaned low in his throat and fixed himself comfortably. He got on his stomach and tossed one of her legs to the side, and the other one to the other side to open her as wide as possible. He began sucking and rolling his tongue over her clit. He spelled out the alphabet on her clit before running the flat of his tongue over it. Her legs shook in his hands. Her moans were breathy, and words were choppy. He inserted two fingers inside her slowly. Her hips began to buck as he curled his fingers in her soaking insides. He wrapped his lips around her and let his tongue make fast flicking movements against her clit. She tried pushing his head away but Denzel kept latched on.

"Sto-De-fu-" He didn't know what the hell she was saying

but he didn't care. He felt her rush of fluids inside her as he curled his finger against her G-spot. She let out a strangled cry as she squirted in his mouth. Denzel didn't stop sucking. But she began yanking at his locks. When the pain of it became too much, he finally pulled away, but not before he lapped up all her juices. She pushed him off the way off and turned over as she had a full body orgasm. But Denzel was so amped up he couldn't wait for her to gain her composure. With all that juice spilling from her sweet pussy he couldn't wait anymore. She'd managed to move all the way towards the top of the bed in her convulsions. Denzel went to the side of the bed and yanked her at the ankle pulling her towards him.

"Wait-wait," She moaned still shaking. Denzel yanked off his underwear. The weight of his throbbing erection felt like he was ten pounds heavier. His tip was oozing with pre-cum and sensitive to the touch. There was no waiting. He continued pulling her towards him until her ass was hanging off the side of the bed. He threw her legs over his shoulders and leaned forward pressing them against her chest. Charm tried to push at his hips but Denzel wasn't having it.

"Get ready," He said pushing his tip at her entrance. She pierced her nails into the flesh of his hips as he sunk his length into her slowly. Denzel felt his eyes start to go to the back of her head. He knew there was something different. She was lusher than she was before. She was wetter. She was dripping with so much juice and still so tight. He felt like his shaft fit perfectly within her, and he was just made for her body.

"Oh my god," He breathed as he pulled out and pushed back in. Charm's head tossed back as he began pumping into her.

"What'd you do?" he asked. "Your pussy feels…"

"Yoni steam," She gasped clawing at him. Denzel dug deeper loving that wet sound her insides always made when he was within her.

Charm was delirious with pleasure. She still hadn't regained her composure from the way he sucked her soul out of her body, and now his thick shaft was drilling a hole through her G-spot. To say this was sex was an understatement. Her orgasms were limitless. She couldn't stop. Even if she tried, Denzel's purposeful strokes wasn't going to let her. As if having an outer body experience, she could hear herself screaming out in pleasure, her hips bucking again as the pleasure became too much. Charm exploded again, feeling the fountain of her release jet out into Denzel's stomach. He was no longer inside her, but Charm could still feel him stroking. Could still feel the plummeting of his shaft against her sensitive walls. The string of curse words that left her mouth sounded like one word. With her eyes closed, she felt Denzel turning her over by the hips. She was placed on all fours and the blunt head of his cock pressed at her opening. She was so sensitive at just that touch she was jetting more of her release on him. He ran his tip against her folds to get her to relax. When he entered her again, Charm didn't even feel like she could hold herself up. She laid her chest flat on the bed with her ass high in the air. Holding her at the hips, Denzel began stroking her again. It was slow, sure strokes that made her legs tremble.

Denzel wasn't going to last much longer. Her walls were quivering, and pulsing around him and it just made him weak. In that moment all Denzel could think about was spilling his seed inside her. His mind ran rampant with the thought of filling her up to the point where he could give her a baby they could name Storm. Just like she wanted. With the way she arched her back, Denzel fell deeper and deeper in her tightness and he began losing all control. She clawed at the sheets underneath him and sang with pleasure.

"Don't stop!" Charm begged. Tears stung her eyes with the intensity of her orgasm.

"If I don't stop Charm you're going to get a pussy full of cum," Denzel gritted. She felt him trying to pull out to hold back his own release but she was on the crux. She couldn't have him stopping. She began tossing her ass back forcing him to stay inside her.

"Charm," He grabbed her ass to get her to stop but it was no use. A woman in the throes of passion didn't stop for anything. And he let her take her pleasure. She screamed in ecstasy and drowned his shaft in cream. Denzel yanked is softening penis out of her just as his own release began to spurt out. He coated her plump bottom with the product of his gender. In that moment, Denzel felt a blissfulness that he'd never experienced it before. But before he could even dwell on how good it felt, everything just came crashing down.

"Denzel!" He heard the shrill scream. But it didn't come from Charm. Denzel felt his heart plummet to the ground when he turned and saw Gabrielle standing in his bedroom doorway. She had her hands over her mouth as she saw without censor what he was doing with Charm's body. Charm froze, taken by surprise. For a moment all she could do was stay still until it snapped in her head that someone had walked in on her and Denzel having sex. She pushed Denzel away from her and grabbed at the bedsheets to cover herself. Denzel stood up straight. There was nothing close to hide himself with, but then it felt ridiculous to hide. Gabrielle wasn't just any woman. And she'd seen him naked plenty of times.

"How the fuck did you get in here?!" He barked at her. Gabrielle stood shock still. She had a feeling Charm and Denzel were fucking but to actually see them in the act just put a whole new reality to the situation.

"Gabby!" Denzel shouted. Gabrielle looked at Denzel. The pleasure she saw on his face was unlike anything she ever saw, even when he was inside her body.

"You're taking another woman?" Gabrielle asked him softly. Denzel shook his head. He went to his drawers and found a pair of shorts. Once he had it on he looked back at her.

"You still have my key," Denzel said realizing he'd never asked for the key back to his place. He held out his hand.

"Give it back," He said. Gabrielle shook her head. She turned her attention to Charm.

"Have you no shame?" She snapped. Gabrielle was depressed at home again constantly wondering how she was going to get her man back. Every time she closed her eyes to sleep she had that awful dream again with that faceless child who was chocolate skinned like Denzel had had those little spikes of locks. Gabrielle didn't know what else to do but she wanted to see him.

She knew something was different the moment she opened the door and she was greeted with the candles. But after just two minutes in the loft, her heart sank when she heard the hysterical moans. She should have just turned and left. But hearing someone be pleasured by her man had her clawing to find out who. And of course it was Charm.

"What are you talking about?" Charm asked.

"Your husband is laid up after being shot and you're here fucking my boyfriend?" Gabrielle snapped.

"Don't pull that card on me," Charm said. "You don't know shit about me." Gabrielle tried to advance towards her, but Denzel stopped her.

"Gabby I told you that I can't talk to you right now. That I don't wanna be with you. Why do you keep calling me and showing up? And then for you to come here uninvited?" Denzel knew he wasn't talking to the same woman he'd been with for years when he saw the tears cloud her eyes and her bottom lip tremble.

"I had that same awful dream again," she whispered. "And you didn't answer your phone. And I- I was so scared. I'm sorry I just came here but I thought if maybe you would tell me like you used to that there's nothing to be afraid of." Denzel sighed.

"I can't do that for you all the time Gabrielle. I told you that we're broken up. And I meant that." Gabrielle sucked up her tears before they began to fall freely.

"Okay fine, you're broken up with me. But are you so sure she's broken up with her husband?"

Charm snuck out of the bed and began putting some clothes on. She grabbed a t-shirt and wiped Denzel's come from her ass then found some clean clothes to put on. She wasn't going to stay here stuck in this drama, feeling like she was a chick from around the way getting caught in bed with another woman's man. Charm didn't need that right now.

"That's between us, okay?" Denzel said. "Now come on, you need to go. Give me my key."

"She doesn't have to go," Charm spoke up. "Because I'm leaving." Denzel turned and realized Charm was basically already dressed and ready to go. After the way they'd just fucked each other Denzel wasn't just going to let her walk out.

"Sit your cute little ass down," Denzel ordered her. He snapped at the bed. Charm stood defiantly and crossed her arms. Denzel went over to her and grabbed her by the elbow and pulled her to the bed. He pushed her to sit down.

"After the way we just fucked each other you ain't going nowhere. Get undressed and relax," He told her. After seeing that she wasn't going to get up again, Denzel turned away from her and headed back towards Gabrielle. He took her by the elbow too and led her out of the bedroom and kept walking towards the front door. He blew out the candles on the way there and flipped on some of the lights. The mood he had with Charm was completely ruined.

"Give me my key," He demanded. Gabrielle slowly handed over the key to his loft. He opened the door and waited for Gabrielle to leave but she never did.

"If you're trying to get back at me, you've succeeded. I'm learning my lesson."

"You think that's what I'm doing Gabrielle? Just trying to

teach you a damn lesson?"

"Why else would you be laid up with another woman? Fucking another woman when it's only ever been me and you? No man has ever touched me intimately Denzel. And I thought that you would keep our pact going until we were able to find our way back to each other again."

"I don't think you're getting that we might never find a way back to each other. I didn't break up with you because your aborted Gabrielle. I broke up with you because you want things out of me that I'm not ready to give you."

"Is it crazy of me?" Gabrielle asked. "To want the man I love, the man I've been dedicated to for ten years to be my husband? To tell me he wants me to be his wife? How long do you think Charm's husband waited before he married her? Am I just that disposable to you?" Denzel actually felt a pang of guilt. He knew most women didn't wait ten years for their man to propose, but this was different. Gabrielle had her flaws.

"Please don't turn this on me Gabrielle," He said. "Do you really think a wife shouldn't support their husband when it came to his work? That a wife would appreciate what he does have and not look down on it. You hate staying here Gabrielle, won't even spend the night but you want us to be married?"

"That's right I've said those things," Gabrielle shook her head. "It was all with a good heart but said completely the wrong way." Denzel crossed his arms. He sighed and shut the door. He figured if he didn't let her get this off her chest she was going to keep coming back no matter what.

"The abortion-"

"I don't want to talk about that," Denzel said. "I'm giving you the chance to tell me what the hell is going on in your damn head but I told you I don't want to talk about the abortion right now. Not unless you wanna see the incredible hulk." Gabrielle backed off immediately noting that he was actually warning her against his anger. She hugged herself and shivered. It wasn't until then that Denzel took actual note of her. She was thinner than usual and again she was wearing a pair of jeans, and a simple T-shirt. Her hair was pulled back from her face again and it was clear in her features she was actually miserable.

"When was the last time you ate Gabby?" He asked her, sighing. She shrugged her shoulders slightly. He knew she never had problems with eating before and she always remained healthy, but after their breakup and the abortion he figured she was thrown off her rails. Even if he was nowhere close to forgiving her, he still found the piece inside him that cared about her. Like he said before, just because they weren't dating didn't mean he could just lose all feelings for her. And in those ten years all he did was care for her and that wasn't something that went away easily.

"I need an answer Gabrielle," He said softly.

"Last night," She replied lowly.

"What are you doing to yourself?" he asked shaking his head. He motioned over to the kitchen. "Sit around the table." She took a deep breath as if relieved he wasn't sending her away. Shaking his head some more, Denzel walked by the kitchen and went back to his bedroom where Charm was still sitting on the bed. She had taken her pants off, only leaving her t-shirt.

"Is she gone?" She asked. Charm already knew something was up because he took a moment to answer.

"No, she's still here," He answered finally. Charm started to rise out of the bed. "No, relax," Denzel said.

"Relax? You want me to just lay here like everything is fine? You just fucked the shit out of me and now your freaking ex is in the other room! Are you crazy?"

"I just need to talk to her," He said. "Or well, she wants to talk to me. And if I don't let her say what she has to say she's going to keep coming back and I just want her to stop!"

"Well then you should do that when I'm not here Denzel! Oh my god I feel like I should be guilty for sleeping with you because of the way she looked at me!"

"Don't feel guilty! I don't!"

"That's so easy for you to say!"

"Charm please. I'm just going to talk to her and give her something to eat. She's starving." Charm shook her head.

"Then I should just go. I'll give you time alone."

"But I want you to stay Charm. You know, I supported you with going to see Terrell in the hospital and even when you sat there crying for him after he got shot I didn't feel the need to just up and leave you." Charm gasped and glared at him.

"Seriously?" She asked. "How can I help support you right now Denzel? Go sit around the table with the two of you and tell her I know how she must be feeling and it's okay to be sad? Tell her that

I know why she misses you because I just got to spend an amazing evening with you? That we came back here and you fucked me like I've never been fucked before, so I can get why she can't move on?!" Denzel crossed his arms. Sure it sounded terrible, but he really didn't want to run Charm off. But she was pulling her jeans on again.

"Listen, I get it. You two need to talk. After a breakup you have to clear the air. I am fine with that Denzel trust me! But don't ask me to stick around, waiting for you and her to have your heart to heart. I would never ask you to stay while me and Terrell talked about our past relationship issues. Me and him still have to have that talk that you and Gabrielle are having right now, so I get it. But I won't stay for it."

"I hope you know that this was just random. And it doesn't determine how I ultimately feel about you or anything," Denzel said.

"I know that Denzel. But respect my choice to leave. It's an uncomfortable situation for me to just stay in."

"I get it," He sighed. Denzel rubbed his eyes. He was two seconds away from spilling his seed into her before he actually pulled out, and instead of rolling over and falling asleep in her arms, she was dressed to leave because his ex-girlfriend showed up. To say their night went to shit was an understatement.

Charm grabbed her purse and grabbed her car keys. It felt strange for her to drive her own car again. Before she left the room she stopped and looked at him. He was still shirtless and his locks were strewn all about his head from her yanking on it. Her legs were still weak and she tried to appear strong but she had to admit it was taking all her strength not to fall over. She envisioned her night ending in his arms with her lady parts sore, but singing that happy tune. And instead she was too embarrassed to stick around because of his ex.

"Where are you going to go?" He asked her. Charm shrugged as they walked out of the room.

"Probably just go back to the gallery. I think I can use a paint session anyways."

"I know you can baby girl but I actually don't want you to go there because you might end up sleeping there. I want you in a warm bed tonight."

"I bet," Charm mumbled. She took a deep breath as she was about to walk by the kitchen to get to the front door. Gabrielle was sitting at the table quietly with her hands folded. True to what Denzel said, she did look as if she hadn't eaten in days. The light illuminated her weary features. She surely wasn't the woman who'd confronted Charm before. Charm just kept her head forward and walked to the door.

"You heard what I said right Charm?" Denzel asked.

"Yeah," Charm responded. Before she walked out, Denzel grabbed her by the arm softly.

"You sure you want to leave?" he whispered. Charm nodded at him. "At least give me a kiss." Charm wanted to kiss him bad. And she was going to walk out without doing so until Gabrielle spoke up.

"Have a good night honey," She said in a teasing manner. Charm glared at her for a moment before she looked at Denzel. She remembered faintly when Brianna told her she needed to grow some balls. Even though Brianna was talking about the way Terrell spoke to her, this was a good way to still stand up for herself.

"Oh I had a very good night," Charm finally spoke. She looked at Denzel and wrapped her arms around his neck. He held her around the waist and met her halfway, kissing her deeply. At first it was just to make Gabrielle jealous but once she started to kiss Denzel she got completely lost. Even if things were completely ruined now, she would never forget how good of a time she had with him. That was something she didn't take for granted. Because now she knew more about the man that was penetrating her body than she did when they first met.

"I should go," Charm whispered. "I'll see you tomorrow." Denzel held onto her tight and Charm had to literally yank herself from his hold. She gave him a longing look before finally turning around and leaving. Denzel watched her get into the elevator and then she was gone. Denzel sighed and closed the door. He turned and looked at Gabrielle feeling resentful. But he was the one who invited Gabrielle to stay because he cared too much.

"Sorry I ruined that for you," Gabrielle said lowly. Denzel wasn't sure how he should respond, so he didn't. He went to the kitchen and looked through the fridge. He didn't have any cooked food to give her so he pulled out the variety of cheese in his fridge. He had a loaf of sourdough bread that he cut a few slices of. He added all four of the cheeses, plus slices of tomato.

"It's not much," He mumbled as he turned on his stove and

got out his skillet. Once it was warm enough he placed the bread on the skillet to toast it until the cheese was melted.

"I always love your grill cheese sandwiches," Gabrielle replied her stomach grumbling. After about ten minutes he placed the hot sandwich in front of her. Gabrielle was so eager to eat she picked it up without realizing the heat.

"Ouch," She sucked on her bottom lip that was burned from the cheese.

"Wait a minute," Denzel said pulling the plate away from her. "Give it a second." He went back to the fridge and poured them both some Iced Tea. Once he sat across from her he pushed the plate back towards her. She began to eat again, but this time blowing on the hot sandwich. She ate at an even pace proving she was actually hungry.

"If you think starving yourself and running back here for me to take care of you is the way to get me back then you got it all wrong," Denzel informed her. She looked up at him and swallowed hard before reaching for her glass to take a sip of her drink.

"That's not what I'm doing," She replied lowly. "I just honestly didn't have an appetite and I didn't know I was hungry until now." Denzel didn't answer her. He just continued to watch her eat. When she was halfway done, she finally came up for air and took a long gulp of the Iced Tea.

"Better?" He asked her.

"Yes. Thank you," She smiled at him. Again, Denzel had a flashback of when they first initially started dating and her smile used to brighten his entire day. Throughout the years her smile sometimes seemed forced and other times she point blank didn't smile unless of course she wanted something from him. But that smile she had in high school, Denzel hadn't seen it until now.

"So talk to me. What you wanna tell me." She took several deep breaths.

"I realize that the way I spoke to you, and what I demanded out of you and even some of the things I said wasn't really the right way to do things."

"You think?" Denzel scoffed. Gabrielle sighed hard. Denzel thought he'd finally provoked her anger and she'd return back to normal. Her anger was provoked but it wasn't the anger he was used to. It was completely different, and yet again he was shocked.

"I know!" She snapped at him. "Ten years and I was

probably the worse girlfriend a woman could ever be to her man! The thing is, I didn't know how bad I was. I took advice and followed everyone else's way about how to be a good girlfriend instead of finding my own way or even talking to you about it!" Denzel was speechless. That gave Gabrielle ample space to keep talking.

"When I told you that your art isn't a real job I didn't mean that your passion for art was invalid. I wanted you to keep working in your art but I thought that maybe if you were an art teacher in a school it would benefit the both of us because you'd have the consistent check coming in. I mean now of course since you dumped me I got to reflect on all the dumb shit I said to you when I really didn't mean it and I just feel so awful."

"It wasn't just my job," Denzel finally spoke. "You never wanted to stay here. Like this loft wasn't good enough for you."

"It is," She said softly. "It was my indirect way of telling you if we moved someplace larger then we could possibly start a family."

"You can say that now? When you had my growth inside you and you fucking killed it?!" Denzel smashed his fist against the table. She jumped and backed up, fear springing to her eyes. Denzel took a couple deep breaths and tried to calm down. He couldn't afford getting angry with her. Because there would be only two outcomes. He'd either put his hands on her or he'd fuck her. And he wasn't interested in doing either of them. He felt his nose flaring as he tried to calm down.

"I want you to take your anger out on me," She spoke. "I deserve it."

"You know what I would do to you," Denzel said. She knew well because in ten years he'd had to exercise his anger somehow. And instead of hitting her, he'd tie her ass up and fucked her until she spoke in tongues.

"I don't mind it," She whispered. "What you do to me." Denzel leaned forward.

"I just had my dick in another woman," He said. She sighed.

"I know. But I-I just want to give you whatever you want. I just want you back." The desperation in her voice was also new. And the sincerity of it scared Denzel down to his bones. Maybe the break up was a wakeup call for her and now she was ready to change her ways. But was it too late for that? He didn't want this dilemma.

"You're running to her because of all the things I deprived

you of. All the things that you needed that I failed to give you. I can't fault you in that. Only myself." Denzel remained quiet. Gabrielle yawned and he saw her eyes start to get low.

"But as you said maybe it'll take you a while to even think about forgiving me for what I did."

"Looks like you're tired," Denzel finally spoke.

"Please don't ask me to leave," She whispered. Denzel's brows went up.

"So you'd volunteer to actually sleep here?" She just simply nodded. Denzel sighed hard for what seemed like the 100th time that night. Charm wasn't going to come back even if Gabrielle left.

"I feel like every time I close my eyes I'm going to have that horrible dream again," She admitted.

"So you haven't actually been sleeping?"

"No," She sighed. Denzel shook his head and rubbed his eyes. He hoped he didn't regret this.

"You can stay," He spoke. "But we're definitely not sleep on the same bed."

"That's fine," She said lowly.

"Finish your food," He said getting up. He left her in the kitchen then went back to the bedroom. He blew out all the candles that were still burning. The scent of hot sex was still in the air when he went into his room. He could smell Charm's perfume. Exhaling slowly, he stopped thinking about the heated night he just spent with Charm and began cleaning up the room. He cut off the music then stripped the bed of its sheets. He opened the window to eliminate some of the heat before proceeding to make his bed with clean sheets. When he was finished and the room was back to normal, he carried a new pair of underwear with him to the bathroom so he could take a shower. He was a little wary because he figured Gabrielle would use this time to try and sneak into the bathroom with him. So he washed himself thoroughly but quickly. He was quite surprised she didn't try to come into the bathroom by the time he finished. He dried off in the privacy of the bathroom then put on his underwear, before he left. He went back into the bedroom and expected Gabrielle to be on the bed but she wasn't there. He pulled his locks from the ponytail and let them fall all around his face. He walked back towards the kitchen but she wasn't at the table either. The plate she'd eaten out of and their glasses were cleaned and drying on his dish rack.

"Gabby?" he called out. There was no answer. He left the kitchen and went to the living room where he finally found her on the couch fast sleep. She'd taken her clothes off, so she was laying there in only her panties. She never wore a bra to sleep so he wasn't surprised at seeing her chest bare. She was curled into a fetus position since she hadn't retrieved a blanket. Denzel watched her for a little bit before he went back to his bedroom to get her a blanket. It belonged to him, but it was one of her favorites because of the texture. So when he returned and wrapped it around her body she sighed in comfort and snuggled deep into it.

Denzel was restless for the whole night. Like a creep he sat in the chair across from the couch and just watched Gabrielle sleep. He was confused as to why he let her get back into his life this easily. He swore he was still pissed at her, and he was. But seeing her in need and looking so affected by their breakup made him want to care. For her to acknowledge her mistakes and how she could have been a better girlfriend was a real big step for her. Gabrielle was never apologetic. Not like this. Sitting back and watching her sleep it made Denzel wonder if ten years was too long for him to give up. If Gabrielle changed completely, and she was the woman he fell for then things would be harder for him to decide what to do. Because in the back of his head Charm was a consistent thought. There was just something about her that he wanted. And it was that spark from the first day he'd laid eyes on her that was still within him. That had to mean something too.

Since Denzel was nowhere close to being tired, he went for his sketchbook and began doodling and drawing random things. He was still sitting across from Gabrielle watching her sleep. When she sighed and began turning over, Denzel thought she was waking up, but she only fixed her arms in the blanket, pulling it down a little. Her breasts popped out as she turned she lay on her back. Denzel didn't move an inch. But looking at her sleeping face, his wrist began moving and before he knew it, he was drawing a rough sketch of his sleeping ex-girlfriend. Once the rough outline was done, Denzel finally stood. He gave her one last look before he turned off the lamp and retired to the bedroom to finish the drawing completely.

Chapter Fifteen

Charm sat in front of the gallery in her car. She knew she told Denzel she felt like she should have a paint session, but now she didn't feel up to it. The only reason she was still there was because she didn't know what else to do. She didn't want to bother Jason or Brianna to come keep her company when it was getting late. And really, Charm was thinking about what Denzel and Gabrielle were doing alone. Why'd she have to leave? But staying there would have made her feel uncomfortable and more so, she didn't want to become like Destiny. Inserting her presence when it wasn't needed. Gabrielle was well aware of her and Denzel's relationship. So to be there hanging around for a conversation that had nothing to do with her seemed too petty. And she understood that long relationships were hard to end. Hell, she had her own issues with a husband she didn't want, but legally still carried his last name.

"Get your life together woman," Charm scolded herself. Since she couldn't sit out in front of the gallery she had to make a decision of what she wanted to do. She would have chosen Jason without thought at any other time, but having the day she had with Brianna earlier was what inspired her to call Brianna first. Jason would always be her best friend, but having another female to hang out with was also refreshing.

"If you're calling me something must be wrong," Brianna said when she picked up her phone. "Because after all that candlelight me and Jason left that place you should feel like a damn princess." Charm chuckled.

"Well, everything was fine and it was all great. But then Gabrielle showed up. It looked like they needed to figure some things out so I left. I would have called Jason but I thought I could come and hang out with you. If that's okay."

"Of course it's okay. I'm watching Netflix and I can pop some popcorn. Come over."

"Thanks Brie. See you soon." Charm felt relieved. She hung up the phone and headed straight over to Brianna's place. Brianna was outside waiting for her when she pulled up. She parked on the street just a few spaces down.

"So did Denzel make you leave to talk to her or?"

"No it was my choice to leave. It just felt weird being there with her. And he said she was going to keep showing up if they didn't have a talk so I thought they should get some privacy. Denzel was actually begging me to stay. I just couldn't."

"I told your behind to grow some balls Charm."

"And I did! Gabby was trying to tease me so I gave Denzel a deep ass tongue kiss right in front of her before I left."

"Good job," Brianna smiled at her. They went up to her loft and the smell of popcorn filled Charm's nose. Brianna gave her a pair of shorts and a t-shirt before going to the kitchen to get the bowl of popcorn. Even though her night took a completely different turn, Charm felt good lying in bed with Briana, giggling like school girls as they ate popcorn and watched 'She's gotta have it,' on Netflix.

****

The next morning, both women work up energized. While Brianna showered, Charm did her hair in the mirror and they both sang like they were in concert opening up for Beyoncé. Charm received a good morning text from Denzel, but that was it so far. She didn't mind his distance now because they'd all be at the gallery within the hour. They needed to prepare for their paint and sip session happening the next day. They had enough people coming to their sessions, plus classes, to make a good amount of the next two weeks. Charm was happy that all three of them wouldn't be in the hole and it was worthwhile that Denzel and Brianna came to work with her. With three individuals they were able to have larger classes which mean more profit for them.

Brianna and Charm got dressed and without eating they headed towards the gallery. They drove in separate cars since Brianna was going to have to head to a violin lesson after her time at the gallery. But on their way to the gallery they stopped to get breakfast and coffee for everyone. When they arrived at the gallery only Jason was there.

"Where's chocolate man?" Jason asked. "Fucked him to death Charm?" He teased. Charm rolled her eyes but a smirk came to her face.

"He should be on his way I guess," Charm replied. "We didn't spend the night together, so I don't know."

"That's a whole 'nother story," Brianna said when she saw Jason about to ask what happened. He shrugged and helped them bring in the food and the coffee. But while the three of them ate and expected Denzel to be coming in at any minute, he didn't. Charm didn't want to seem as if she was getting worried so she didn't mention it to the others. But inside she was wondering why he hadn't shown up yet or texted any of them. They were supposed to meet at 10, and time filtered on without him there.

"I guess we're starting without him?" Jason asked. Charm checked her watch. It was past 11 now and they'd been there waiting for an hour.

"Well let's just get some of the tools prepared for the event and wait until he comes to have the meeting about upcoming work. Because then we'll have to repeat everything over," Charm said.

"Alright." The three of them went to work getting together the small canvases and paints and paintbrushes they give to the participants to work in. They piled it all neatly in the corner of the room before the task of moving the long tables in place dawned upon then. Neither Charm nor Brianna were too prissy to pull their sleeves up and help move the tables. While Charm and Jason were carrying the last table to its place, Denzel finally stumbled into the gallery.

"Sorry I'm late!" he blurted out. He saw Charm straining as she was helping move the table. He immediately hurried over to her and took the table out of her hands and continued to help Jason.

"Nice of you to show up," Brianna exhaled. She was breathing heavy from just lifting the last table with Jason.

"Sorry. Just had a long night," He mumbled. When he had retired back to his room he had literally spent the whole night adding color and shading to the drawing of Gabrielle. He still was a little restless but when he finally went to sleep it was in the early morning hours. He woke up to the smell of food and music. Once he caught a glimpse of the time he'd hopped out of bed and tried to rush to get dressed. What shocked him the most was the fact that when he went into the kitchen Gabrielle had made him a full course breakfast. He'd dropped everything in his hand that he was holding when he saw the spread on the table. He didn't have any groceries to begin with, but she'd woken early to go grocery shopping and to come back to make him breakfast. He didn't know how to react to it but his stomach was growling so he sat there and gobbled food down as quickly as possible. He thought she was going to start preaching to him again about being together but she was quiet as a mouse. And after she cleaned up, she redressed and was ready to leave. She thanked him for allowing her to stay the night and then she was gone. Denzel didn't know what had gotten into her but that wasn't his girlfriend. At least that wasn't the girl he broke up with.

But now he was at the gallery late with Charm looking him up and down. He thought she was going to say something and he was prepared for it. But it was when she just hummed and turned away that he wasn't prepared for. Even Brianna was giving him a look. And he knew when his best friend was angry to tease him and when she was actually angry with him.

"You could have let us know that," Jason spoke. Even he wasn't his usual happy self.

"Sorry I was just trying to get here. Did you guys have the meeting?"

"Nope. We were waiting on you," Brianna said. Denzel looked back at Charm. She still hadn't said anything to him and her face was too placid. He didn't know what she was thinking. She must have felt some type of way because this was her company and when it came to her events she was serious about it.

"There's still some food left if you're hungry," Brianna told him.

"I'm good. I ate," He said lowly. Charm shifted uncomfortably and she didn't mean for him to see it, but he looked directly at her.

Jason took charge instead. They all sat on beanbags and discussed the events that were coming up and what they would need to have for each one. For now Jason had them booked for a couple events and each of them were looking at good money within just two weeks. Charm finally spoke then and informed them she wanted to try to book bigger events and jobs to increase their income. Everything was interesting but all Denzel could do was look at Charm. She didn't even give him a glance and he knew that wasn't how she would usually react to him. When their small meeting was over and everyone continued to set up Denzel pulled Charm to the side.

"Let me talk to you," He said.

"Denzel we have to outline some of the canvases with the image for the paint and sip tomorrow. That's a lot of work to get done."

"I know that Charm. But I want to talk to you." She looked towards Brianna to help her make her decision. Brianna nodded and waved her hand telling Charm to go and talk to him. Charm exhaled.

"Fine," She pouted. She led the way to the office where he closed them inside. She leaned against her desk and crossed her arms.

"I didn't intend to show up late," He said.

"No one intends to show up late for something," She replied. "But you must have had a good night and slept pretty well."

"What's that supposed to mean?" he asked her. She just shrugged. "You know, I asked you to stay last night and you didn't. So don't come at me like that."

"I can come at you how I want to Denzel. This is my freaking company! The least you can do is respect me and be here when you're supposed to. I never ask anything out of you and Brianna but to just be here and be present!"

"Respect you?" Denzel asked. "When have I ever disrespected you? I'm trying to apologize at being late. But you know besides this I've never shown you one ounce of disrespect. You let me be intimate with you Charm. I can't disrespect the woman that has been allowing me inside her body." He saw when her facial features began to soften.

"Apology accepted then." He tried to take her hand to embrace her but she evaded his touch.

"What?" He asked her. "If you're not upset me then I do want to kiss you." She gave him a strong look.

"Charm just say what you're thinking," He demanded.

"Did you sleep with her?" She blurted out. Denzel's eyes went wide in his head. "Because you're never late to things. And then you spend the night with her and then you show up late saying you'd already eaten as if she's been taking care of you all night and morning." Denzel shook his head.

"You think I'd do that do you?" he asked. Charm shrugged.

"Well I didn't think Terrell would have cheated but guess what?"

"Yeah well guess what else? I'm not your damn husband. I would wait at least a day before sticking my dick in someone else. So no we didn't have sex. And you know what she did to me Charm. You think I'm interested in being intimate with her?" Now Charm felt like an idiot.

"I'm sorry," She sighed. "That was dumb of me to accuse you. And you're right. You're not Terrell." She was ready to leave the office then but he took her arm and pulled her close to him. He wrapped her arms around his neck and held her. He inhaled her sweet scent. Damn he really missed her and it had only been one night. Not to mention he was so restless because his girlfriend was sleeping on his couch.

"I don't mean to snap at you," He whispered. He began placing small tentative kisses on her neck. She arched for him so he could get a better angle. Oh his lips felt so good. While he kept kissing she reached one of her hands down to palm his growing erection.

"Did you miss me when I left last night?" She asked breathily.

"So much," He groaned, pulling her flesh into his mouth and sucking on it. Charm's eyes fluttered close. While her hand went to unbuttoning his jeans and reaching in for her prize, his hand went under the skirt that Brianna had lent her. His finger easily moved her panties over and dipped inside of her.

"That Yoni Steam still has you that luscious huh," He said. Charm inched back so she could look into his face.

"You felt how powerful that steam was," She smirked.

"With or without it baby girl you feel amazing." He began thrusting his finger in and out of her.

"We can't do this right now," She gasped. "So please stop. I just wanted you to get a feel." But he didn't listen.

"Den-remember the outlines we have to do for the-" A moan cascaded from her lips when he added a second finger. She pressed at his chest.

"Alright, I'll stop," He said easing his fingers out of her. He brought them to his lips and sucked off her juice. He was actually going to let her go until he tasted her. He cursed under his breath and decided then and there he wanted more. He picked her up and carried her to the bathroom and shut them inside.

"What are you doing?" She shrieked.

"If you aren't loud they won't hear you," Denzel teased. He set her on the counter and pushed her skirt up. He left her panties there but just drew it to the side.

"No, Denzel we can't! We shouldn't do this here! This is our place of work!"

"I'm not gonna penetrate you baby girl, relax. Don't tell me you've never done anything sexual out of your house before."

"Well, I haven't," She admitted.

"First time for everything," He said. He went into his pocket and pulled out a small peppermint candy, unwrapped it and tossed it into his mouth. He sucked on it for a few minutes before opening her legs and setting them at the angle he wanted it. Charm watched with her stomach rising as falling as he bent over in front of her and used the tip of his tongue to lick the seam of her lips. She caught a chill at the teasing feel of his cool tongue against her warm center. He spread her lips slowly, gazing at her as if he couldn't believe what was in front of him. He took her all in before using the flat of his tongue and running it up and down her pink insides completely. He left the trail of his minted saliva behind on her aching clit. He blew his cool breath against her.

"Sto-stop teasing me," She said shakily. He gave her a wicked smile before diving in. He took the tip of his tongue and rolled it across her clit slowly like waves. She was nervous about doing this here at first, but now she had given over to the pleasure and she was gone. Her head fell back as her mouth slowly fell open. He held her lips open cleanly so nothing got in his way as he flicked and sucked in her clit. He found her spot right under and hood and licked at it like a cat lapping at milk. Charm felt her back arch as she started to cum. Again she was pulling at his locks.

"I'm about to cum," She mewled. He drew at her flesh, making loud popping sounds as he sucked her harder. But it was when he started nibbling on her sensitive clit that was her undoing. Her hips flew in the air as she came hard. He made slurping sounds, vibrating his lips around her clit. He left the mint directly in her clit and held her legs open, holding her down. The mint felt like it was melting against her clit. Her legs was still shaking. Again, this wasn't supposed to be anything more, but seeing her shaking with her orgasm, Denzel couldn't just leave her there. He cursed and pulled his penis through the zipper of his jeans. He kept the mint on her hot clit and pulled her down to the edge of the counter. His entry inside of her was smooth and he buried himself to the hilt in one thrust. He grunted in pleasure as her walls surrounded him in lush heat. He began pounding into her. Forget being quiet. When he was inside her, everything else around him evaporated. There was nothing else to concentrate on but being inside her tightness and thrusting into her until their bodies became one. Again, his balls were clenching and he had to question on whether he wanted to fill her with his cum or not. She just felt that fucking good.

"You're gonna make a mess," She moaned out. Already she knew when he was about to come. She would feel him begin to swell and his thrusts would become frenzied.

"Don't worry about me," He grunted. He tapped the flat side of the peppermint stimulating her clit once more. Her body began to shake again, but he wasn't hitting her G-spot like he wanted to. And even though they'd only just begun to have sex, Denzel knew when he was giving it to her the right way and when he wasn't. He grunted in anger and pulled out of her. She tried to grab his shirt to pull him back but he moved out of her reach. He sucked up the peppermint from her clit pulling at her sensitive flesh softly until she was coming in his mouth again. The peppermint was virtually gone so he just bit into it and ate it. He picked her up from the counter and placed her against the wall. Her side was against the wall, but she turned her upper body a little to face him. He knew she was flexible enough for the act, so he lifted one of her legs in the air and held it against his chest. Her eyes went wide as his swollen dick found her entrance and entered her again. Charm's eyes rolled to the back of her head and the leg that was supporting her still on the ground was shaking like a leaf. Denzel felt when he'd hit her spot. He smiled wickedly.

"That's it ain't it?" He asked, wrapping his hand around her neck. She clawed at his clothes as he thrust into her evenly. He grinded in her, tearing her guts up like it was nothing.

"Shitttt," She screamed feeling her plateau getting nearer and nearer. Through her low lids, she gazed at Denzel. His face was strained as he pumped into her as if he didn't want to bust before she did.

"I want to come inside you so bad," He grunted punching the wall next to her head.

"Don't!" She begged as she finally reached her plateau. She wanted to give him that warning because the moment the words fell from her mouth, she was lost. Everything was blank as his thick dick finally ran her into an orgasm. The orgasm was so powerful no words left her mouth even though her mouth had flown all the way open and in her head she was screaming. Her eyes were shut tight as her body seized up.

"Fuck Charm," Denzel grimaced as she creamed all over him coating his chocolate colored dick into vanilla. She finally let out a small moan as her body floating back down to earth. Her eyes opened and gave him a dazed look.

"Come for me now," she whispered. And that's all it took. He pulled his dick from within her. In one movement her leg was down and she was squatting in front of him swallowing him whole. He felt his toes Crip walk, and his eyes cross as she sucked him. His seed jetted out in less than 2 seconds, and she gulped it down like it was chocolate milk. Denzel had to grab to wall or he'd fall over on her. She licked and rubbed his shaft up and down until he was completed depleted of every last drop. She popped him out of her mouth and looked up at him. That innocent smile she gave him made his body tingle. It wasn't like Gabby's smile that had him infatuated with her when they first met. Charm's smile was completely different. And the genuineness he felt when he saw her smile just made him warm. He pulled her to stand and held the back of her head, plunging his tongue deep in her mouth. She mimicked the action. For another five minutes they stood in the bathroom kissing sloppily. The fact that you could kiss someone so deeply even after the orgasms were done meant that there was much more to your relationship.

But once the dirt settled they realized they'd really just had hot and steamy sex in the bathroom of the gallery. That's when they started to laugh. They helped each other clean themselves up and correct their clothing. Charm used wet wipes to clean herself and then wipe down Denzel's shaft. When she held his heavy manhood she felt a sense of ownership. And it was dangerous. She gave him a look and he seemed to understand exactly what that look meant. Once they cleaned up they both took a deep breath and left the bathroom.

"How long we been gone?" Charm wondered. But she didn't even think that mattered. Jason and Brianna weren't stupid. And Charm knew endless teasing was about to ensue. Denzel went ahead of her and opened the office door. Both Brianna and Jason fell inside shouting as they hit the ground. Charm gasped realizing they must have been leaning against the door to try and hear what was going on. On the floor, they held each other and laughed before slowly getting up.

"You got fucked didn't you?" Brianna asked with a wide grin on her face. Charm just smirked and held her head down.

"I told you!" Brianna said to Jason. "20 bucks!" Jason sucked his teeth and went into his wallet and pulled out the bill and slapped it in Brianna's hand.

"You bet on my vagina?" Charm gasped. "Really guys?"

"Jason started it. He said you wouldn't have sex in public. I said, if Denzel flashed his little ding a ling at you, then you would."

"It is not little," Charm corrected her. She moved her jaw from left to right. "My jaw hurts and I only sucked for like a minute before he popped." That statement left Denzel, Jason, and Brianna with open mouths.

"Come on guys, we have a lot of work to get done!" Charm smiled at them and walked out of the office first. Denzel closed his mouth and took off after her.

"She's fucking sexy ain't she?" He said, following her like a lovesick puppy.

Chapter Sixteen

When Terrell opened his eyes he smelled Destiny's cheap perfume. He groaned and grimaced with the pain that always met him when his meds wore off. It didn't help that instead of being greeted by Charm he was being greeted by Destiny. He blinked the blur away from his vision and looked towards Destiny. Apart from the pain in his body, seeing Destiny looking like she'd drank herself to death and then rolled out of a dumpster before coming here have him more pain.

"Destiny," He groaned. She looked at him.

"Good morning," She greeted. Terrell turned his head away from her rank breath.

"Jesus what'd you do? Gargle sewage water?" Destiny crossed her arms.

"Excuse me?!" She snapped.

"Your breaths smells like ass Destiny! Get out of my face!" Destiny moved away from the bed. After her night out with Gabrielle she hadn't even been back home. She's been at Terrell's side the whole time and that meant her own hygiene was dwindling. But that's where he wanted her right? At his side every minute.

"Well you were knocked out for another day I thought your ass was about to slip into a fucking coma so I didn't leave your side. And this is how you talk to me?" Terrell sucked his teeth.

"You see the way Charm keeps herself?" He asked her.

"Why the hell you asking me about that little slut?" Destiny asked. Terrell sat up and raised the back of his bed.

"Don't call her a slut! And I'm asking you about her because you know she keeps herself properly groomed at all times. And that's my wife. So you should have an idea of the kind of standard I keep. So if we gonna be around each other Destiny, and if it's my baby in your damn belly you gonna have to start keeping yourself a certain way. This ain't cutting it," Terrell said waving at her.

"Fine then. I'm gonna leave. But Charm looks the way she does because you pay for her to. Do you think anyone is paying for me to get my hair and nails done? I don't have new clothes or-"

"Just take my wallet and go shopping and do whatever the hell you need to do," Terrell cut her off. He knew this was coming sooner or later. And he didn't mind putting out of pocket for her to look good. Because like he said, she was going to be in his life and carrying his child. He needed her to look a certain way.

Destiny went back to the table next to his bed and took up his wallet. He showed her what card she was able to use.

"Why this one?" He asked.

"Because it's my card. The other ones belong to me and Charm. And if you go swiping it, she's gonna know I'm spending more money on you." Destiny rolled her eyes. Terrell put his hand in her face to stop her from what she was about to say.

"You gonna stop calling her names and talking shit about her," Terrell said. He held his ribs as the throbbing of pain continued.

"I just don't understand why you won't just let her the fuck go. She made it clear she doesn't want you. I'm the one carrying your kid. The kid she by the way can't give you."

"She's still my wife. When she gets over her little temper tantrum then she's going to come home. Which means you're gonna need to know how to act when she's around. So you need to stay in your place and she'll stay in her place."

"You expect me to live with her?" Destiny asked. "Newsflash Terrell I'm not sharing you with anyone. So if you bring her back home just know that I'm going to leave and you're never going to see your baby." She opened her phone and flipped through her gallery until she found the photo Gabrielle sent her the night before. She turned over the phone then showed it to Terrell.

"There's your prissy little always up to standard wife," Destiny spat. "Being fucked behind by another man while you're laid up in here half fucking dead." Terrell grabbed Destiny's phone. He glared at the picture of Charm. His wife. With pleasure blended into her face that another man was giving to her. Terrell shouted in anger and threw Destiny's phone across the room. If not for the protective case it was in, he was sure it would have shattered against the wall.

"Are you crazy?!" Destiny shouted at him. She ran to the other side of the room and picked up her phone, examining it. She gave Terrell a hardened look.

"The sooner you come to terms with reality the better off the both of us will be." She gave him one last look before turning around and leaving the hospital room so she could go shopping and get her hair done.

Terrell sat there alone and in pain. He grunted as he tried to switch positions. He felt like he'd been on his back since he got admitted. He took his phone off the table and looked at it. He was ignoring all his office calls and clients. The word went around that he'd been shot and in critical condition at the hospital but not one of his coworkers had come to see him. The office had just emailed him detailing that he was to take as much to recover as needed. They worked off commission so there was no paid time off. So unless Terrell got his ass up out of this hospital and started selling homes again then he would be out of his consistent income.

Shaking his head, he closed out all those messages and emails that had nothing to do with him. He stared at the wallpaper on the screen of his phone. Charm's face was smiling back at him. In a flash, he remembered how her face looked when she was being pleasured that by that fucktard who was trying to take her away from Terrell. Grunting, he opened his Facebook app and went straight to Charm's profile. Unlike before, her page was flooded with pictures. But none of them were picture's she'd posted. It was Jason who'd taken pictures of her at the gallery with that fucktard, and another woman and tagged her in the posts. Terrell just looked at the photos of his smiling wife and he felt his heart beginning to sink. What would he do if he ever lost her? Terrell couldn't even think of being without her.

It was after 5pm, and even though he'd been sleeping for what seemed like days, Terrell was still tired. And he just wanted to go home. Charm didn't take his calls but that didn't mean he didn't stop trying to call her. And so that's what he did. He listened to that same monotone ring before her sweet voice came through.

"Hi this is Charm! Sorry you missed me! Leave a message after the beep!" Terrell chuckled at the sound of her voice. But slowly his chuckles turned into sobs as he realized how deep of a hole he'd dug himself into. He just wanted his damn wife back. Just as he went to press the dial button again, his phone vibrated in his hand. Charm's photo popped up on the screen. She was calling him. Terrell wiped his eyes and hurriedly answered the phone.

"Charm," he whispered.

"Terrell," She replied. Her tone wasn't full of disdain and it was sweet. It wasn't like anything she'd been giving him since he woke up.

"How-how are you?" he asked choppily.

"I'm okay," She answered. "Working as usual. How are you?"

"In pain," He replied honestly. "But I just want to go home." Terrell heard laughter coming from her end of the phone.

"Baby girl the food is here!" Someone shouted. She moved her mouth away from the phone.

"I'll be right there!" She called out. An envious heat filled Terrell. He wished he was back at home with her, having dinner.

"Sorry," She said coming back to the phone.

"I know you're busy but um, I just wanted to hear your voice," Terrell told her. Charm was quiet not knowing how to respond to him.

"Are you still there?" he asked.

"Yeah, I'm here," She spoke up.

"I know it might be much to ask but I wanted you to come see me again."

"After what happened the last time?" She asked.

"It'll be different this time. Destiny isn't here and I'll tell her not to come back for now. And if you don't bring that man then it'll just be me and you talking." Charm was quiet again.

"Please Charm," Terrell begged. Charm could hear the sob in his voice and it appalled her. She suddenly felt empathetic.

"I'm stuck here in this bed and I just want to see you Charm. Please." Charm rubbed her eyes.

"I'm gonna have dinner then I'll come see you," She spoke finally. "But if Destiny shows up. I'm out of there." The relief that soared through him made his pain almost nonexistent.

"Deal," He said quickly.

"See you." And then she was gone. Terrell immediately reached over and pressed the call button for his nurse.

"Mr. Robinson how do you feel?" She asked.

"My wife is coming," He said excitedly. "I want to get a shower." He tried to get up but the nurse stopped him.

"I'll give you a sponge bath. We don't want you up walking around yet." Terrell groaned. He knew the nurse had been giving him sponge baths but he longed for a hot shower. Where he could feel the water cascading off his tired and aching bones.

"Fine," He snapped. The nurse left the room and came back moments later with a basin and gloves. She closed the door then helped him get out of his gown and his underwear before she filled the basin with warm water and soap. Even if it wasn't the shower he wanted, the warm water and sponge did feel good on his skin. The nurse cleaned him thoroughly before moisturizing his body with the lotion Destiny had brought to the hospital from his home. She helped him put on clean underwear and then another gown. He gritted his teeth through all the pain of his movements. She checked his wound and made sure no signs of infection had settled in.

"I'll get you some pain meds," She said.

"No! They make me too drowsy. And my wife is coming I need to be awake when she does." The nurse didn't like that he was denying the meds but she just nodded before leaving the room. There was nothing she could do if he didn't want to take his medicine. But she was happy to see that he was excited for something and not so depressed.

The elevator doors opened but Charm was stuck. Everyone else in the elevator filtered out, but Charm didn't move. The doors closed her back in and that's when she realized she needed to make a move. She pressed the button to open the doors again. And when it did, she took a deep breath and stepped out. After having their late lunch, Charm told Jason, Brianna, and Denzel she was going to see Terrell. They of course was unsure about her decision and Denzel was ready to go with her. But this time she felt she needed to go see Terrell alone. So she bucked up and headed to the hospital. The only reason she'd called Terrell back in the first place was because she knew that she couldn't keep ignoring him. They were going to have to talk at some point. But after the time she was having with Denzel nothing bothered her. She felt carefree and she felt this happiness that she didn't have when dealing with Terrell. So here she was in the hospital ready to see exactly what he wanted. She was wearing the same thing she had on earlier at the gallery but when she stood in the doorway of Terrell's room, his eyes went wide as if she was wearing something straight off the red carpet or something. He sat up some more and an eagerness in his features that Charm hadn't seen before was there.

"Charm," He smiled. Charm stepped into the room and closed the door behind her. She could smell the men's Vaseline lotion that he always wore. Charm stood at the end of the bed.

"How you feeling?" She asked him. Terrell stared at her. The glow on her skin was blinding him. He couldn't stop looking at her.

"Terrell," She snapped her fingers. He blinked and smiled at her.

"Sorry," He said. "I just can't believe you actually came." Charm raised her arms and dropped them to her sides. The door behind her opened and the nurse came in with Terrell's dinner. Charm moved out of the way and let her take the food over to him. The nurse smiled and left promptly.

"You can sit next to me you know. I don't bite," Terrell told her. To prove she wasn't afraid to be near him, Charm went to the chair next to his bed and sat down. He pushed his tray of food away and just looked at her.

"I missed you," He said. He attempted to reach for her hand but Charm moved her hand away from him.

"We need to talk about how this divorce is going to go Terrell. I don't mind packing all my things and leaving the house to you. All I want is the car and my gallery. If we settle things peacefully then we won't have to go to court and drag any of this out." Terrell shook his head.

"Charm we can't divorce," He said. "I refuse to lose you to this." Charm shrugged.

"You have a family to worry about now Terrell," She sighed. "You wanted a baby and now you got one. I'm just not going to stay with a cheat." Terrell shook his head. Up till this day he had no recollection of sleeping with Destiny the first time that resulted in her pregnancy. And even if he sought out in his brain the events of that night, it just wasn't coming back to him.

"Charm, I don't know how it happened," Terrell tried to explain. "I came home, I was upset that I didn't get the sale and Destiny-she told me to have a drink and just relax. And so I did. I took one drink and then I don't know I black out after that!"

"But you knew you'd had sex. Because you kept asking me if we'd done anything."

"Because my dick was sticky! And I knew if I had sex that it would only be with you. I wouldn't sleep with anyone else!"

"Until a month later when you were fucking her willingly up a wall," Charm responded. Terrell was stumped. He felt himself breaking down internally.

"That was the worst mistake of my life," He said lowly. Charm just looked at him. His head was down as if he couldn't bear to look at her.

"Was it?" Charm asked. "You don't regret cheating the first time?" Terrell finally looked at her. His eyes were watery.

"I regret it all," He breathed. "I don't know what I was thinking, what I was doing. I didn't intend for Destiny to be pregnant like that. I just wanted us to have a baby Charm. And she just-she kept testing me and like the weak man I am, I couldn't stand it and I gave in. And for all that Charm I am so, so sorry. I know you can't forgive me right now but you have to know that I don't want to lose you." He quickly wiped the tears away from his eyes before they could fall.

"And I guess I deserve this right?" He questioned looking at her.

"Deserve what?" Charm asked quietly. Terrell looked down at his chest where he knew his wound was.

"Whoever tried to shoot me should have just put a bullet in my heart," He said ominously. Charm shook her head immediately. Even though he did break her heart she wouldn't wish death on anyone. That just wasn't in her nature.

"Don't say that Terrell!" She urged this time she reached out and touched his hand. He took her hand in his warm grip and held it so tightly.

"I'd rather be dead than to be without you Charm," He admitted looking at her. "And I should be dead for what I did to you. For causing you this much pain."

"But you aren't dead Terrell. And you can't think like that. Me? I'll get over it. But you have a baby growing inside someone. So you have to be there for them. If anything that's all you need to think about!"

"You think I want a baby with that woman? I fell under her temptation that's true. But she's not wife material. Not like you. And I can have sex with her a million times and still not want her."

"You don't have to want her Terrell. But you're stuck with her." He rested his head back against his pillows and continued to hold her hand. The sadness in his voice for some reason made her sad. But the reality of the situation was that they had to eventually put this behind them and deal with what was important. Charm was finding solace in another man who made her feel beautiful, and Terrell was having a baby. It was time for them to really move on.

"I don't think I can be happy, baby or no baby if you're not in my life," He whispered. Terrell kept his head rested back against the pillow looking straight up at the ceiling. But Charm didn't need to see his face to hear his sincerity. And she was left speechless.

"Tell me what to do," He said. "Tell me how I can get you back in my life? To get you to stop sleeping with that man and to come home to me?" Charm shook her head hard. She took her hand from Terrell's grasp.

"It's not just about sleeping with him, Charm said. She didn't even know why she felt the need to explain herself to him.

"We have-"

"What is she doing here?" Destiny gasped. Charm backed away from the bed completely. Here she was caught again by another girlfriend or side chick, or whatever the hell Destiny was. Charm didn't like being put in these situations. The one with Denzel was bad enough. And she wasn't going to sit around for the embarrassment.

"Good night Terrell," She said immediately. She started to walk off but Terrell grabbed her hand.

"Wait!" He exclaimed. "Don't leave!"

"We agreed that I would only come if she wasn't here. So now I'm leaving." She pried Terrell's hand from around her wrist and headed for the door.

"Running off to get back shots again?" Destiny teased her. Charm just glared at her. Her hand was itching to smack fire out of Destiny. But instead she took deep calming breaths.

"Have a good night," Charm told her. She gave her a smile to show that Destiny hadn't gotten under her skin. She took one more look at Terrell before she walked out of the room and hurried out of the hospital.

Destiny turned and looked at Terrell. She couldn't believe he was doing this behind her back.

"Really?" Destiny asked. "I turn by back and here she is yet again." Terrell rubbed his eyes to get the last bit of tears out of them. With Charm running away from him again, and now Destiny at his ear, agitation wore high in his body and he felt himself losing control.

"Shut up Destiny," He snapped at her. "I told you already Charm was going to be part of our new family and that's just that!" He held his chest as it became hard to breathe. He felt contractions in his chest that he'd never felt before. His felt like his chest was about to explode from not being able to draw in any air.

"Terrell? What's happening?" Without answering her he pressed the call button again. the nurse hurried into the room ready to help him.

"What the hell is happening?" Destiny asked the nurse.

"He's just having trouble breathing because of his rib. Stay back and let us work." The doctor hurried into the room next with another nurse. Destiny backed all the way to the corner and watched them try to get Terrell stable again.

Chapter Seventeen

Saturday evening, the night of their paint and sip event, Charm was blocking all her calls from Terrell. She thought she was doing them both a favor by going to see him but there was no closure, and it only opened the both of them up to more questions. Charm didn't know what the hell to do with Terrell anymore. It seemed that no matter how much she claimed she and him were separated he was never going to just let her go. And even if she didn't want to, she was just going to have to bring their divorce to court and make a scene about it.

But this Saturday was all about the event. She wasn't thinking about Terrell, or dealing with him. So once she had her phone off, she got in the right mindset to focus on what was important. She had spent the night with Denzel again, but after breakfast she went to Jason's home where she did some final things for the event and eventually got ready there. She and Jason were the first to arrive at the gallery, but when Denzel arrived he was carrying to bouquets of flowers. One he gave to Brianna, and the other one he gave to Charm.

"What's this for?" Charm asked smelling the flowers. Denzel smiled at her.

"Just 'cause," He replied. He kissed her on the cheek then walked further into the gallery to start helping Jason pour the wine in the glasses. Charm looked at Brianna.

"Get used to it," Brianna said. "We always reiterate to people that we're not dating but then he shows up with flowers for me, and all this nice shit. Turns out he's just one of those men. I asked him why he does it for me and he said even if we're not dating that doesn't mean I'm not still a woman. And sometimes a woman just deserves flowers." Brianna shrugged.

"That's so cheesy," Charm smiled.

"As cheesy as that smile on your face," Brianna teased. Charm giggled and went to put her flowers in a vase with some water. Yes it might have been cheesy, but Charm really liked it.

"Do you like them?" Denzel asked coming up behind her.

"I love them," She smiled turning to look at him. He pressed up against her behind and kissed her neck.

"I got something else for you too. But that's for later."

"Something like what?" Charm asked.

"Sitting on my face," He replied lowly. He kissed her on the cheek and walked away. Charm was stuck for a minute not knowing what to say. When she turned around and watched him walk away she couldn't help but lick her lips. He was wearing those black pants that fit his ass perfectly with his black V-neck t-shirt and suspenders again. She would gladly sit on his face later then ride him until they both passed out.

"Charm!" Charm turned at Brianna's voice. People were beginning to arrive at the gallery. Charm jogged over to the door. She and Brianna were at the front door smiling and welcoming people as they came inside. Both Denzel and Jason were prepping the wine glasses on a long table where people could go and choose which wine they wanted to sip on.

"I think that's everyone," Brianna said seeing that most of the seats were already taken. Charm was closing the door when someone ran up and held it.

"Sorry I'm late." Charm felt the smile drop from her face when Gabrielle pushed her way into the gallery. Brianna stood there with her arms crossed. Charm could see she was ready to pounce if Gabrielle did anything stupid. Charm stood in between then just in case that happened.

"What are you doing here?" Charm asked as politely as possible.

"The paint and sip is tonight right?"

"Yes. But did you sign up and pay for it?" Gabrielle went to her phone and scrolled through it. She flipped it over and showed Charm the Eventbrite receipt. So she'd paid. Technically Charm couldn't turn her away. She cleared her throat and moved out of the way. Gabrielle gave her a smug smile and strutted over to the table where she could pick up her wine glass.

"Hi Denzel," Gabby said to Denzel. He paused mid motion as he was reaching to hand her a wine glass. He expected it to be another woman and not his Ex. He coughed and gave her the glass.

"What are you doing here?" He asked her. His eyes flickered to Charm who was standing near the door trying to avoid looking over at them.

"Well I paid for the event so yeah."

"Okay but why?" Denzel was confused because she never

wanted to do anything related to art. Ever.

"I decided that maybe I should experience what you love. I think it'll be a good learning experience for me. And perhaps fun right?" She smiled at him before sipping on her wine.

"I guess so," Denzel mumbled. He watched as she sauntered off to the last long table and sat at the end. She was wearing a long flowing sundress that wasn't overly sexual and not that glamorous. She must have went shopping because her new low key wardrobe wasn't anything he'd ever seen her in.

"So we're just going to let her stay?" Brianna asked coming over to Denzel. Charm followed behind her, keeping quiet.

"She paid Brie," Denzel said.

"Did you tell her about this?" Brianna asked.

"No! But I posted it on my Facebook page. So I don't know, she probably seen it somehow.

"I still wanna know what that heifer did to you," Brianna gritted.

"Not now Brie," Denzel shook his head. "It's time to start. Charm take it away." He gave her a nod. Charm refused to let Gabby ruin their event so she put a smile on her face and went about conducting the event like nothing bothered her. With Brianna and Denzel there, they added another dynamic to the event. Brianna had her jokes, and Denzel was there to back her up. Most of the time though the women were just goo-goo eyes over him. In a way it made Charm smile with glee knowing that women wanted what she had. And she didn't have a problem with Gabby either until she started becoming annoying.

Gabrielle thought that being at the gallery would distract Denzel from everything besides her but it was the complete opposite. Since he handed her the wine glass he hadn't even looked in her direction. She was hardly focused on the stupid painting because she was so focused on the way Denzel interacted with Charm. It was ever so subtle but she saw the way he touched her. Gabrielle felt the vein under her eye ticking. She hadn't taken her medication but she was trying her best not to go in a rage.

"Hey Denzel!" She called from the back of the room. He looked towards her. "Can you help me with something?" He looked apprehensive at first before he finally came over to her.

"What's up?" he asked.

"I just have a little trouble getting the outline done. Could you help me?"

"We have canvases with the outline already. Would you like that one instead?"

"I wanted to try it without first. I just need a little boost. Please?" Denzel took his pencil from behind his ear and leaned over her. He continued drawing where she had stopped. He drew a few of the lines before he stopped to allow her to continue. When she made a mistake she shook her head.

"I suck at this," She pouted.

"Maybe a little," He replied. She looked up at him.

"You never had any complaints about my sucking," She retorted. Denzel actually laughed.

"Stop it," He shook his head. "Come on. Try again." She turned back to the canvas and tried to outline the painting. When she began getting off line, he held her hand and guided her the right way. Gabrielle caught real chills when he touched her. Oh show she missed his touched. She missed it so much that she sighed and felt herself leaning back resting against him.

"Don't," He said to her pushing her away softly. Sure enough when he looked up Charm was glaring right at them. He tried to move away but Gabrielle grabbed his arm.

"You know it's never going to work out with her right?" Denzel's brows furrowed as he looked at Gabrielle.

"What are you talking about?" He asked her.

"She's married Denzel! I don't know what she's using you for-well actually she probably just really enjoys the sex. But when it's said and done, she's going back to her husband. And I don't want you to be left alone because of that." Denzel shook his head and took his arm from her grip.

"If I'm meant to be alone Gabby, then I'll be alone."

"But why? When we could be together? When I could be here for you?"

"Because you had your chance Gabrielle," He said. "And things would have been better if you didn't kill-" He cleared his throat feeling himself getting upset again. No. He wasn't going to do this to himself right now. Not again. Instead of saying anything else to her he simply walked off.

Brianna was entertaining the group of women with music, getting them to sing the words to Mary J. Blige while they painted. Since everyone was distracted no one noticed when Denzel snuck off into the office but Charm saw. She slithered off hoping no one was paying her too much attention. In the office Denzel was leaning against the wall with his head down.

"You okay Denny?" She asked. He only picked his head up and gave her a strained smile. Charm ran her hands through his locks and stood in front of him. He leaned his forehead against her shoulder and that's where they stayed for a couple minutes. Denzel didn't need to say anything to her because the comfort of being able to lean on her was just enough for him.

"Thanks Charm," He said to her. He lifted his head from her shoulder and held her at the waist.

"A woman like you is rare," He said. "Just know that." Charm gazed at him wondering what prompted him to say that. She was going to ask when he put his fingers against her mouth.

"Don't question it," He smiled at her. "Let's go back." He took her hand and led her out of the office back into the main gallery.

Gabrielle could feel herself slipping when she saw Denzel and Charm emerge from the office holding hands. When people noticed them of course they let each other go and continued parading around the gallery like they were the hot new 'it' couple. Gabrielle tried to break them up again by calling out for help once more. Denzel turned to look at her but it was Brianna who walked to the back towards her.

"What you need?" She asked politely, but Gabrielle could see the cold calculation behind her eyes and she knew Brianna wasn't about to play around with her.

"Just wanted to ask how it was looking," Gabrielle murmured.

"It looks great! Keep up the good work!" Brianna said sarcastically. She gave Gabrielle a 'don't fuck with me' face before walking off. Gabrielle sucked her teeth and continued painting. She kept an eye out for what Denzel was doing during the whole event, and on several occasions, Gabrielle caught him staring at her. She'd smile at him and he would only make eyebrow movements at her before looking elsewhere. She knew Denzel for a long time and she knew that when he wasn't particularly happy but not particularly angry at something he'd move his eyebrows in a way to give some sort of facial expression. For some reason it gave Gabrielle comfort because at least he wasn't pissed at her. Those facial expressions were never pleasant.

Instead of trying to get his attention anymore she just relaxed and painted. With the music on in the gallery, Gabrielle found herself feeling like she was in the twilight zone or something. She was actually enjoying herself. Her painting was nowhere near as good as others but she didn't care. She was actually proud of herself. The calmness that entered her from painting she could use to her advantage. Instead of taking the stupid medication she could use painting as a way to keep herself from going into different emotional instabilities.

As the class ended, the group of women gathered in the front to take a large group photo with their paintings. Gabrielle was apprehensive about being part of the photo but then Denzel looked at her. He said nothing and made no facial expression, but she was just lured to him. She stood next to him tentatively and held her painting, still feeling proud of it. After the photo a few people lingered to speak with Charm, Brianna and Denzel before they got their things to leave. It was overall a really productive night. Even if it might not happen all the time at least Gabrielle knew that there were ways for Denzel to make money and eventually support her in their future.

"I really enjoyed this," Gabrielle said to them. She was the last person there. She'd lingered on purpose not wanting to leave.

"I'm glad," Brianna smiled. " Well we have a lot of cleaning up to do so-"

"I saw on the calendar on your Facebook page Charm that you're having another event like this next week. I think I'll pay to come to that one too. This was more therapeutic than I would have guessed. I see why you enjoy it so much Denzel." He nodded at her but said nothing else.

"Alright, enough of the nice shit. Can you get your shit and go?" Brianna asked. "I'm tired of being nice to your ass," She let out a deep breath as if she was winded.

"Well I was thinking Denzel that I could meet you at your place again? We do still have to have that talk about what happened." Denzel looked at Charm. She was biting her bottom lip tentatively as if her mind was running a mile a minute. When she felt him staring at her she looked at him and shrugged.

The last time Gabrielle butted in, he chose to listen to her instead of sending her away so he could spend the rest of the night with Charm. That wasn't happening again.

"Not tonight," Denzel said.

"Oh, you have plans?" Gabrielle asked.

"I do actually."

"Next time I guess. I'm sorry for what I said earlier too. You didn't deserve that." Gabrielle put her painting on the table closest to her. She didn't know what she was thinking, but she was still on her emotional high from the painting. She felt too good not to go for gold. She walked slowly towards Denzel. He saw her coming and took one step back.

"Don't do that," She smiled. "What you think? I'm gonna stab you or something?"

"Well you got that pennywise ass smile on your face. You look creepy as hell Gabby. What are you doing?"

"Just thanking you," She admitted. She stood in front of him. Looking over her shoulder she saw Charm and Brianna glaring at her. But she ignored them and looked back at Denzel. He was close enough so she could whisper to him.

"You didn't have to allow me to stay here and you did. So thanks."

"Well you sort of paid," He replied. "So yeah it's not like I had any choice." Gabrielle felt her eyes getting watery from his rejection. So much for emotional stability.

"I'm trying," She whispered. "Can't you see I'm trying to make it right?" Denzel was a sucker for tears. Every woman in his life knew that. And no matter how screwed up their relationship got he did have to admit that her new attitude was proof that she was trying to change.

"I see that," He told her. "But like I said, some things aren't easy to get over. And just because you show up to my art event doesn't mean that I'm going to be sweeping you in my arms and carrying you off in the sunset after what you did. So understand that." She wiped at her eyes and nodded.

"Okay fine. I get the picture." With his guard down, Gabrielle leapt up and wrapped her arms around his neck. She hugged him tightly but he didn't wrap his arms around her.

"Gabby," He warned. "Get off me." She looked into his eyes.

"I just miss you so much," She sniffled. "Just let me hold you for a minute." Denzel couldn't even imagine how he looked right now with his ex-girlfriend clinging onto his neck when the woman he was falling for was just a few feet away from them. He didn't even want to look over at Charm. He felt so embarrassed. He tried to get Gabby's arms from around him.

"Stop it," He said. Just as he got her arms from around his neck, she lunged her head forward and kissed him.

Now it was Charm's turn to feel like she was in the twilight zone. Everything went in slow motion when Gabby's lips touched the lips of the man she loved to kiss. Next thing Charm knew she had Gabby around the back of the neck yanking her away from Denzel. Charm continued to hold Gabrielle by the back of the neck even though the woman flailed around. Things started back up and returned to regular speed. Charm blinked her eyes. For an instant she almost regretted putting her hands on Gabrielle but then she let that shit go. She didn't care if Denzel wasn't her man yet. She was going to let her territory be known. Denzel wasn't just a simple fuck to her. Destiny being pregnant was one thing. She wasn't going to let another woman walk all over her. And this time this woman didn't have a fetus growing in her, so she was all game.

"Are you crazy?" Charm asked Gabrielle. "No seriously? Did you lose your mind?"

"Denzel tell her to let go!" Gabrielle begged.

"Don't say shit," Charm snapped at him. "You lucky I only have my hands on your neck and not tugging at your damn hair." She dug her nails into Gabrielle's neck.

"You know," Charm started. "I'm here tryna be classy and shit. Tryna show that women ain't all claws and no flaws. I'm tryna be the bigger woman in the picture but for some reason you and the chick my ex knocked up just be trying me like I can't get ratchet. Like I can't hang up my classy panties and beat a bitch down." Charm made Gabrielle look at Denzel.

"You see him right there?" Charm asked. "Answer me." She squeezed Gabrielle's neck.

"I see him," Gabrielle whimpered.

"You had your chance. So you gonna move on, and give the next woman a shot to show him some real love. So until he tells you that he wants you back that's all mine sugar. From the top of his head to the birthmark on his ankle, that's all me. I'll let you slide this time. But come around him again and act a fool if you want to. I'll drag you up and down this gallery until I got biceps like Popeye." She pushed Gabby towards the door finally letting go of her neck.

"You'd let her do that to me?!" Gabby shouted towards

Denzel. But Denzel didn't have an answer for her. He just blinked and looked at Charm. He'd never seen her like that and though they weren't official there was just something about seeing her fight for him. It meant she saw them going somewhere.

"It ain't about what he gonna let me do," Charm said stepping in her face. "I respected you when you were dating him. Hell I saved you from getting your front teeth knocked in after you did what you did to him. So what I'm not gonna do it allow you to come up in here disrespecting me. You caught us red handed with me on all fours and him balls deep inside me. So you know what we doing. So don't come around trying to hug and kiss on him again. I promise you Gabrielle you not gonna like the woman I become if you touch him like that again. Get the fuck out of my gallery."

"I can call the cops on you," Gabby whispered.

"Hold up you want to use my cell? I'll dial it for you." Charm reached for her phone.

"I'm not joking," Gabrielle stammered.

"And do I look like Kevin Hart?" Gabrielle shook her head.

"You just need to go back to your fucking husband and leave me and Denzel alone," Gabrielle snapped. "Instead of finding out who shot him you riding the next man's dick. Have you no conscience?!"

"What I have is multiple orgasms from riding said man's dick. You mad?" Gabrielle's face turned beet red.

"I'll get you Charm," She gritted. "Smile and shit now but you just wait. Next time I won't fucking miss." She snarled at Charm before turning and storming out of the gallery. Charm almost felt like running after her and asking her what the hell she was talking about but Brianna tugged on her arm and turned her around.

"Finally! You grew that pair I kept telling you to grow!" Brianna cheered. "Way to tell her off for touching your man." Charm looked at Denzel.

"Let her touch you like that again and I'll A-town stomp on your dick," Charm warned pointing a finger at him. Denzel bit his bottom lip.

"Can I talk to you in the office real quick?" He asked. Both Jason and Brianna sighed hard.

"We both know what that means," Brianna said. "Why don't ya just take her home instead of giving her an office quickie?"

"Mind your business," Denzel snapped. "You coming

Charm?" He asked walking towards the office. Charm saw the lust in his eyes and when he bit his lip again she lost it. Her skin was scorching with arousal and her panties were slowly getting wet with her liquid gold.

"Yeah I'm coming," Charm said following after him. She looked at Brianna who winked and gave her the thumbs up. Charm smiled and turned away to continue after Denzel.

"Aye," Brianna called out to her. Charm turned back around to see something flying at her. With fast hands she caught the small item before it hit her in the face. Charm looked at the Listerine strips then back at Brianna confused. Did her breath smell?

"Oh for shit's sake, suck him off with a strip in your mouth," Brianna rolled her eyes. "Do I have to teach you every fucking thing?"

"Oh," Charm laughed. She slapped her head feeling silly. "Got ya," She said holding the strips tightly and turning back towards the office. Denzel was waiting at the door for her. He gave her a heated look as she walked by him before he locked them in the room alone.

Chapter *Eighteen*

Denzel flopped down in between Charm's breasts, trying to calm his breathing. She was mewling in delight as her orgasm ebbed out slowly. The sun was rising over the horizon sending morning rays through Denzel's bedroom window.

"I have got to stop giving you some every day," Charm breathed. "You're going to get spoiled."

"I'm afraid it's too late," Denzel said. He fixed his body between her legs so he could stay laying between her breasts and not have his weight crushing her. He felt her running her fingers through his locks. After their consummation in the gallery office Denzel couldn't wait to get her back to his place so they could go for a second round. But what turned into seconds, turned into thirds, and then next thing he knew the sun was coming up.

"My poor vagina," She teased.

"Your poor vagina? What about my balls? Do you know how hard it is to hold back when all I wanna do is bust and you're clenching the shit out of me? And I know if I give in, you'll give me one of those disappointed 'can't believe he came before me' type looks. And I simply can't deal with that kind of disappointment." Charm burst out laughing and held him tightly.

"If I don't clench you're going to feel nothing." Denzel rolled his eyes.

"You know that's not true." They went quiet for a moment.

"What made you act out against Gabby last night?" Denzel asked. "Like you said, you normally keep it classy even if Brianna has been telling you to grow some balls."

"Was it unattractive?" Charm asked him. "To act like that?"

"I wouldn't have been so eager to get inside your body I had to have you in the office again if it was Charm," He said. "It really turned me on in fact."

"Well I bet Gabby has probably gotten all territorial like that about you before."

"Not like that."

"I know we're not a couple Denzel, but look at us. You've been in my body more times in week than my husband has been in a month. And I don't know I just feel like if I can't fight to get you then I can't fight to keep you."

"So you know how I said our sex wasn't meaningful?" He got up on his elbows and moved up her body. His rising erection was aching to be inside her again.

"Denzel I'm sore," She whined pressing at his abdomen.

"Relax baby girl," He said kissing her pouty mouth He slid inside her slowly not wanting to irritate her aching walls, but to massage them. She moaned and threw her head back.

"You remember when I said our sex wasn't meaningful right?" he asked again.

"Yes, I remember," She breathed. "Kind of hurt my feelings but I understood what you meant."

"Seeing you get like that over what we could potentially have in the future makes me realize that none of this wasn't meaningful. It just meant that I was only seeing our sex. I wasn't seeing what we meant to each other." Charm hissed, drawing in a ragged breath as he pushed against her sore G-spot. Wasn't she lucky to have a sore G-spot?

"And just knowing you want to fight for me now makes me want to be with you even more."

"I wish-I wish I could give myself to you," She moaned.

"Listen…" Denzel breathed. Charm shut her mouth and heard the soft slushing sound of their bodies blending together.

"Sounds like you're giving yourself to me," He said.

"You know what I mean," She mewled. "I wish I wasn't Charm Robinson. Because if I was just Charm Bradley, you'd be my man Denzel. You'd be all mine." Her mouth opened in a long moan as she hit her climax. Denzel grunted and pulled out of her before he filled her with his release. They both gazed at each other, panting.

"As long as I have you in my arms right now Charm, then I won't have to worry about when you'd be my woman. I don't mind the journey baby girl. Because the destination is worth waiting for." Slicked in sweat, and tired from round after round of passionate sex, they embraced in a sloppy tongue kiss further mingling their bodies into one entity. When they pulled away from each other Charm pushed a stray lock from his face.

"Did you hear what Gabby had whispered to me?" She questioned.

"Actually I didn't. What'd she say?"

"That she was going to get me. And this time she wasn't

going to miss." Denzel's brows furrowed.

"She said that to you?"

"Yeah! I don't know what she meant but I haven't stopped thinking about it. And she's never tried to like hit me before or anything so I don't quite get what she meant by she won't miss this time."

"As long as she doesn't touch you Charm," Denzel said wiping her damp hair from her forehead. "Let Gabby be Gabby."

"Fine," She smiled. "Now can you take me for a quick shower? I can't feel my legs." Denzel chuckled and got out of bed slowly. He couldn't feel his damn legs either, but he carried her to the bathroom and they showered together. This time, they were both too depleted to think about anything else but getting clean and getting back in bed. So what if it was 6 in the morning? Denzel was gonna sleep until he didn't know what sleep was. Charm didn't even stop to put on any clothes. She dried herself and fell into the bed snuggling under the covers.

"Close the curtains," She groaned groggily. Before getting under the covers himself he shut the sun out of his bedroom bathing it in darkness.

Charm was deep in sleep before she felt Denzel come in bed next to her. Her dream came quickly, falling over her like a heavy blanket. Instead of a big comfy bed next to Denzel, she was in an open field filled with crying babies. Everywhere she turned she saw crying babies.

"What the hell?" Her voice sounded hazy and far away but it was still hers. She looked around at all the crying babies but she couldn't pick any of them up. So she just walked. She didn't know where she was going until she heard a different kind of cry. It was the same wailing sound but to her ears it stood out more than any of the other babies. She turned in circles until she found the baby the cry belonged to. Something about the baby called out to her. She felt her feet moving quickly as she rushed towards the small human. Unlike the others when she bent over and touched the child her hand didn't go through it. Charm quickly gathered the baby in her arms. He immediately stopped crying. Charm got lost in his round chocolate eyes. It took her a moment to realize that none of the other babies were crying anymore. She looked around her and the field was gone. Her breath caught as she was standing in a room she didn't recognize holding a small child that was snuggled up to her chest.

"Hi baby," She said lightly, feeling as if the words came to her naturally. "Hungry?" She rocked the child in her arms.

"Let's get you some mi-"

"Mommy, mommy!" Charm looked up from the baby in her arms to the two little toddlers who ran into the room she was standing in. They were only about two years old and could barely walk without falling over each other. Charm noticed that the pair of them were twins. They were rolling on the floor laughing with each other and repeatedly calling her.

"Mommy, mommy, mommy!" Confusion filled her as she looked down at the baby in her arms. When she made eye contact with the infant a sharp pain pierced through her stomach.

"Not again!" She screamed.

Denzel jerked awake hearing Charm scream. She was grabbing her stomach and looking down between her legs as if searching for something.

"Charm, baby girl stop," He said grabbing her wrists to get her to calm down. She stopped screaming and looked at him. The fear in her eyes made his heart hurt.

"What's the matter sweetie?" He asked.

"I-I-dreaming and there was this baby and then twins and I felt my stomach in pain, just like my miscarriage and I-"

"Sshh," Denzel hushed her and brought her close to his body. "Are you pregnant right now sweetie?" He asked.

"No," She breathed.

"Then don't be afraid of a miscarriage right now. It was just a bad dream."

"But the twin babies, I-I was never pregnant with twins so I don't understand why I was dreaming of-"

"Dreams are not meant to be understood sweetie," Denzel said. He made her lay down but still held her close, spooning her. He rubbed his hand over her heart to get her to calm down.

"I'm so sorry you had to go through that," He said kissing her cheek and her neck. "I'd do whatever just to take that pain away from you." Charm felt her bottom lip trembling as she thought about losing all four of her babies. Denzel felt her warm tears on his arm. He thought he was a sucker for tears until Charm cried. His heart began to crumble.

"Please don't cry," He begged holding her tighter. "You

know I'd do anything to make you happy right?" Charm nodded.

"If you want me to Charm, I'll give you another chance to have a baby." He heard her gasp before she sniffled and wiped her eyes and her nose. She turned in his arms until she was facing him.

"You'd do that for me?" She asked. Denzel just nodded. She was tempted to get more of her fertility medication and letting him come inside her until she was able to have his baby. But then she remembered that he only knew of one of her miscarriages. Not all four. He didn't know she couldn't fulfill her natural role as a woman.

"It sounds too tempting," She spoke finally. "But I just want to spend my time being with you Denzel. Like you said if we make our destination then we can start another journey into being parents. You don't have to feel obligated to knock me up because of my miscarriages."

"I'm not obligated," He said simply. "Don't ever think that." Charm leaned her head on his chest and closed her eyes. He kissed her again before they both drifted back to sleep in the safety of each other's arms.

****

Gabrielle sat in her car outside of Denzel's place feeling like shitty leftovers. After the night at the gallery she'd went to his place and parked. He'd taken his key away from her so she was planning to just wait for him to get home before convincing him to let her stay at his place again. But when he arrived home, he didn't arrive alone. Charm was trailing behind him in her car. He waited for her to park before she got out all giddy and sucked his face off for five minutes before they went inside. And there they stayed. Now the sun was completely up and the hustle and bustle of the day started and neither Charm nor Denzel made an appearance. Gabrielle couldn't sit there all day looked like a degenerate so she finally left. But she was getting tired of playing this game with Charm.

"You have those drugs yet?" Gabrielle asked when Destiny picked up her phone. She was agitated without having anything else to do but if Destiny had her drugs it would make her feel better. Even if she was iffy about being pregnant and doing that to her body, it might be the only thing he could do to get Denzel back.

"Yes I got it. It was expensive though. I hope you have the money."

"Whatever. Where you want me to meet you?"

"Come by my place. Or well the place that used to belong to

Charm." Destiny ran off the address before Gabrielle hung up. She headed straight through town to Charm's large home. To think the woman went from this place to being satisfied with Denzel's little loft was mind boggling to Gabrielle. She began to wonder just what Terrell looked like. He must have looked good to have a woman like Charm in the first place. And if Charm was the one frolicking in paint all day, then her husband was probably the one with the money. And by the looks of it, he had a lot.

"Welcome to my place," Destiny greeted opening the door in a short robe.

"Is the husband here?" Gabrielle asked.

"No. He's still in the hospital." Destiny pulled out a small draw string velvet bag. Before she gave it to Gabrielle she waited for her payment. Gabrielle shoved the money in her hand and snatched the bag.

"You're in a bad mood this morning," Destiny said.

"Last night I went to Charm's art event so I can get close to Denzel. It was almost working until that bitch had to come ruining everything. And she spent the whole night at his place."

"They were probably making love all night," Destiny said. Gabrielle wanted to cock back and slap Destiny for even saying it. But she just clenched her fist.

"You sure you don't need some drugs to mellow out?" Destiny asked her.

"What I need is Charm out of my damn life and away from my damn man!" Gabrielle gritted.

"Well I don't got no damn ideas! I tried to get her ass arrested but that didn't work out." Gabrielle snapped her head in Destiny's direction.

"Wait what?"

"The cops still don't know who shot Terrell. I tried to tell them that Charm did it so she'd get locked up but that didn't hold up. There was no evidence." Destiny watched as a wide smile came over Gabrielle's face.

"I know who shot Terrell," She said.

"Who?" Destiny asked.

"I did," Gabrielle shrugged. Destiny backed up going towards the knives just in case Gabrielle was on some kind of serial killing mode.

"Relax," Gabrielle rolled her eyes. "I was aiming for Charm

and I hit Terrell."

"What you telling me this for now? Unless you plan on killing me!"

"Because now I know how to get rid of Charm! You tried to get her arrested but didn't have any evidence. I'm the one who shot at Terrell, so guess what I have in my possession?"

"The gun?" Destiny realized then the plan that was formulating. "You're going to plant the gun on her possession and the cops will have evidence! Wait, how?"

"The only place where she can't argue that anyone could have planted it is her car. I break in her car, put it somewhere where she can't see while she driving, call the cops and tell them I saw her with a gun. They'll test it and know that's the gun that shot Terrell and boom. She's in jail." Destiny pointed at her.

"Fuck breaking in. She has a spare key." Destiny went to the key hook and took the spare car key she knew belonged to Charm's car. She tossed it to Destiny.

"Text me when you plant the gun. I'll call the cops and tell them I saw her with a weapon and they'll come investigate."

"Then Denzel is all mine," Gabrielle hummed. She couldn't wait. "I'm doing this today," She exclaimed. "I'm through waiting around for my man."

"I'll be ready!" Destiny said. Gabrielle gave her a high five before scurrying to the front door. Her morning started off with her full of agitation, but not elation was in her bones. The prospect of getting Denzel back was in her reach.

She raced home to retrieve the gun she had hidden away afraid that it would be the thing that implicated her. But instead of her, it was going to implicate someone else. And that cleared Gabrielle of the crime she committed in shooting Terrell, and the crime she was going to commit to get rid of Charm by shooting at her again.

Chapter Nineteen

Charm sat on Denzel's kitchen counter watching as he cooked dinner. She insisted that she should cook for him but he just wanted to cater to her. She'd been at his place nonstop since the event and he wasn't interested in telling her to leave. And whenever she did try and go to Jason's house he would literally block her from leaving. It was almost a week since the event and she hadn't been this happy. She felt like she never wanted to leave his place. They went to work together in the morning and went back to his place every night. Charm honestly felt they were a couple but knew in her heart they couldn't be just yet. She'd sent texts to Terrell begging for a peaceful divorce but that wasn't going to happen.

"And then just a pinch of salt," Denzel sprinkled salt on the meat he was cooking. Charm laughed at the way he did it as he tossed the meat around in the pot.

"Maybe you should be on master chef or something," She teased. Denzel scooped some of the gravy so she could taste it. No matter how she teased him it actually tasted real good.

"Yummy," She smiled. Denzel leaned over and licked gravy from the side of her lips.

"That's not all that's yummy," He said. Sadly, Charm had begun spotting so she feared her period was coming so they hadn't been making love since the event. It was tough only because he turned her on so much but it wasn't like sex was the only thing that made them interested in each other. Not having sex made their relationship prove that it was real.

"Don't even start," She pushed at his chest. He backed up and returned to his pot.

Two loud bangs at the front door startled Charm. She hopped down from the counter and immediately stayed at Denzel's back.

"Police! Open up!"

"Oh no," Charm whispered.

"It's okay baby girl. Go put some clothes on." She was only wearing pajama shorts and a tank top so she hurried to the bedroom to put on sweats and a t-shirt. Denzel answered the door while she was gone.

"You again," Denzel said to the detective that wanted to

arrest Charm.

"Where's Charm?" He cut straight to the chase.

"Why?" He shoved a warrant in Denzel's face.

"To search her car. She can either come open it for us or we're breaking in." Charm came out from the bedroom and walked slowly to the front door.

"Why do you need to search my car?" She asked.

"Another tip. Let's go." Charm shrugged.

"I've got nothing to hide." She shoved her feet in her shoes and was ready to lead them downstairs. Denzel cut off the stove and followed them. He didn't understand why they kept getting tips leading to Charm when she was innocent in all of this. They really wanted to pin this on someone.

Outside, Charm pressed the open button on her car and stood back while two officers rummaged through it. Denzel wrapped an arm around her and held her close as they both watched the cops. The detective glared at Charm and Denzel as if he detested the very ground they walked on. But he didn't even know them.

"Detective. Check this out." One of the police officers came forward holding a gun in his gloved hand. Charm's stomached bottomed out.

"Did you just plant that in there?" Charm questioned the cop. "That wasn't in there earlier when I was driving around!" The detective sighed and opened his file.

"Terrell Robinson was shot with a .22 caliber gun. The exact kind of gun found in your car. Can you explain that Mrs. Robinson?"

"I-No! I don't know where it came from!" She looked at Denzel, but he even looked to be at a loss.

"Has anyone taken your car for a drive without your knowledge?" He asked.

"No, only I've been in it." The detective shook his head and pulled out his handcuffs.

"Wait! How you arresting her for something she couldn't physically have done since she was there in the first place?!" Denzel shouted.

"Well I have probable cause to arrest her for having the weapon of the crime. Unless Mrs. Robinson comes clean and outs the shooter then she'll be taking the fall for the crime."

"Charm Robinson you're under arrest for the attempted murder of Terrell Robinson...." He continued reading her rights in a monotone voice while cuffing her hands behind her back.

"I didn't do this!" She shouted out to him. Denzel was forced to watched as Charm was shoved into the back of the patrol car, fear bright in her eyes. She looked at him through the window as tears rolled down her cheeks.

Denzel didn't know what was going on, but he just knew his Charm wasn't capable of hiring someone to kill someone. Not her. But yet still, again she was in the back of a patrol car being whisked away to a police station. The only difference was that this time she had an attempted murder charge stamped to her sweet name.

To be continued

CPSIA information can be obtained
at www.ICGtesting.com
Printed in the USA
LVHW03s1718180618
581091LV00002B/491/P

9 781720 673620